Smallbrook
By
Gary Cann

Best wishes

Gary Cann

1

Chapter One

The old wagon creaked slowly between the high hedges of the lane, with an equally old horse struggling against its worn harness to keep it moving. Panting heavily, ears laid back on his head, even the slightest slope was almost too much for the aging beast and the speed of the wagon, too slow to even disturb the dust on the dry roadway, reflected its struggle. Two men were sitting on the wagon, the older of the two, puffing on a pipe was a perfect companion for wagon and horse, and was content to let the horse set its own speed, the reins hanging loosely on his knee as he chatted amiably to his passenger. The other man looking stiff and out of place on the wagon seat, was from his appearance much younger, only in his mid-twenties. As they reached the junction of two lanes, just on the brow of the slope, the older man called the grateful horse to a halt and pointed off between more hedges, where the new lane wound its way down into a gentle vale.

"This is as far I go," he said. "Your way lies over yonder."

"Thank you," said the young man, his deep dark voice holding little trace of an accent. He dropped his large bag to the ground and slowly eased himself down after it. "Will you take something for your trouble?" he asked, offering a silver threepenny piece and wincing slightly with pain as his left foot touched the ground and his leg straightened.

"I will not," said the old man kindly but firmly. "Twere no trouble, lad. It were good to 'ave some comp'ny, so you keep your money. I think you need it more than me." He gestured at the young man's leg with an understanding smile. "I'll say goodbye to you and wish you well." With those parting words, he twitched the reins and the old horse responded by once more taking up the weight of the wagon and gently lumbering forwards.

"Goodbye and thanks again," called the young man after him. Picking up his bag, he began to walk slowly along the rutted lane, hard and dry underfoot at this time of year, whistling tunelessly to himself. It was a beautiful afternoon in the early May of 1916, and the sun shone down, warming his back as he walked. A light breeze was blowing and gently rustling the leaves of the trees and hedges. Birds were singing as if free from any cares, although an occasional blackbird squawked out a warning cry from the hedgerow as he approached, continuing until the intruder had passed.

The problem he had with his leg gave him a pronounced limp and a strange gait as he walked. Like many, many others, he'd been wounded fighting in the muddy, bloody battlefields of France. Hit by machine gun bullets in the left leg, which broke the bone and caused severe muscle damage, his wound had proved serious enough for him to be sent home to England. He was one of the lucky ones to have survived and he knew it. While in the hospital and often since leaving it, he thought time and time again of the men he'd seen, some with missing limbs, some shell-shocked or gassed, and some left blind and every day he'd thanked God to have been spared such misery. The thought threatened to cast a grey cloud over the day and he dismissed it and walked on enjoying the walk and the fresh air after the confines of a military hospital.

His destination was close now, the small village of Dalton Combe, nestling comfortably in the valley he'd only been able to catch fleeting glimpses of from the high seat of the wagon. He'd lived there as a child, a time that seemed an eternity ago and he harboured fond memories of that childhood. For some reason, when he was discharged from the hospital, and put on lengthy convalescent leave with no ties and nowhere else to go, it was to Dalton Combe that he'd felt the urge to return, hoping that there he might find some of the peace and quiet that he so badly needed.

The walk to Dalton Combe wasn't a long one, but by the time he started down the fairly steep hill into the village, he was tired and looking forward to some rest. His leg was throbbing uncomfortably and his head was beginning to ache menacingly. He had a vague memory that the pub in the village had rooms to rent and he hoped he was right.

Passing a number of thatched cottages, he soon found himself in the broad market place, looking at the old market cross that he used to play on as a boy. The base formed a seat and resting his kit bag on it, he sat down for a few minutes to ease both his leg and his head. The village was just as he remembered it. The old parish church on one side of the market place, surrounded by its graveyard, the rectory next to it, hidden by a high hedge just by the lane leading down to the bridge over the river, the pub, almost opposite and the village shop and some houses on the third side. More thatched houses, their timbered walls covered with lime mortar, formed the fourth side.

Everything was quiet and he relaxed, happy to sit in the

late afternoon sunshine. Then a bell tinkled, disturbing his thoughts and he looked round at what was a familiar sound. He soon found the source. The door of the little shop had opened and a middle-aged woman had emerged. The shopkeeper had come to the doorway with his customer and was holding the door open for her. As she walked away, with a curious glance in the young man's direction, the shopkeeper closed the door behind her, causing the bell to tinkle once more. Then the blind came down and the shop was shut. The young man stretched his aching muscles and stood up slowly. Picking up his kit-bag, he walked across the market place to the pub.

The door was open, so he walked into the bar. The closest he had ever been to this room before was when knocking on the little window at the back of the building to pick up a jug of beer for his aunt and uncle. Even then, he'd only caught tantalizing glimpses of a mysterious dark smoky room filled with noisy grown-up men and an aroma of stale beer.

It suddenly occurred to him that in those days he'd never considered, in the innocent ways of a child, that he would ever leave the village, but now here he was, back after years away and in a place in which he had never before been allowed. The thought made him smile.

The room was almost disappointing in its normality when he considered how mysterious it had once seemed to him. Gloomy in the late afternoon sunshine, It was like many bars, down to earth enough to make the local men feel at home in their working clothes, but still clean and well kept. It was simple, to serve its purpose, with a number of tables and chairs, benches around the walls and bare wooden floorboards bearing beer stains that countless scrubbings had been unable to remove.

"Can I help you?" a booming voice asked from the other side of the bar, breaking into the young man's reverie. "I hadn't realised I'd left the door open." The owner of the voice looked at the young man standing in front of him, a quick appraisal of both a stranger and a potential customer. Not too tall – he hadn't had to duck his head coming in through the pub's low doorway - but muscular and well-built, with an erect and confident bearing. Short dark well-cut hair was revealed when the newcomer took off his cap and gave a friendly smile that lit up his clean-shaven face. His clothes were simple but hard-wearing, a brown jacket open to reveal a collarless shirt open at the neck. A pair of trousers lighter than the jacket and a pair of well-worn and dusty boots rounded off his wardrobe. All this the landlord took in almost instantly, also noticing a slightly lop-sided gait as the young man walked towards him. There was an air of familiarity about his face which he couldn't quite place.

"I was looking for a room, not a drink," he replied. "Do you have any?" Looking at the man he assumed to be the landlord, he recognised him, but was unable to remember his name. A large, elderly man, he had a jolly, welcoming face and was wiping his hands on a beer stained apron. He noticed the young man looking at it.

"Take no mind. I was busy in the brew-house," he said cheerfully, gesturing at the mucky apron. Many landlords brewed their own beers, usually to recipes they thought safely their own secret, but which were commonly as traditional as the act of brewing was itself. "Now as to rooms, we have two. How long would you be thinking of staying?"

"I don't know. A few days, perhaps more. I used to have relatives here." The landlord's eyebrows rose questioningly.

"Relatives? What's your name, then lad? Mine's Joshua Carter, as it would be rude to ask for yours without telling you mine." He extended his hand, still slightly sticky despite being thoroughly wiped and the two men shook hands over the bar.

"My name's Nathan Holt".

"Ah, Joe's young nephew, what run off to the army." said Joshua. Nathan Holt nodded. "I thought you looked a little familiar. You were in France, weren't you lad?" As they were speaking, despite Nathan's protests to the contrary, Joshua had drawn two mugs of ale from one of the barrels behind the bar.

"Yes, and in Belgium, with the Old Contemptibles". The landlord drew in a short sharp breath. That was the nickname that had been given to the survivors of the British Expeditionary Force, made up of regular troops, which had been rushed to Belgium in August 1914 to support the tiny Belgian army against the massive German onslaught. Initially successful because of its firepower, it had borne the brunt of the fighting and taken a terrible mauling with horrific casualties, being forced backwards by sheer weight of numbers. Over half of the original force had been killed or wounded. Nathan was indeed lucky to be alive. "I was wounded and gassed at Wipers last year," Nathan continued, "and then the Army put me out on what they call convalescent leave." 'Wipers' was the pronunciation given to the battle of Ypres by British troops. He didn't elaborate, but instead took a long sip from the drink the landlord handed him. Joshua followed suit, eyeing him thoughtfully. The ale was delicious and Nathan said so smiling, the smile again lighting up his face but not disguising a haunted look around his eyes which made him look tired.

"Tis my own recipe - and a favourite of your uncle," said Joshua. He paused and looked at Nathan again. "It was a bad business, your aunt and uncle," he finally said. "They were nice people". Nathan simply nodded, with nothing to say. He took a longer sip from his mug.

At sixteen, he'd run away from the village and his aunt and uncle and joined the army. Even after all these years he didn't know what had led him to do such a thing, particularly as he did it without having the courage to tell them. Possibly, he thought now, he never would know. Although he and his aunt had written to each other regularly, there had always been the hurt in her letters and not once in six years had he returned to Dalton Combe to see them. Then he'd received the news that there'd been a fire in their cottage and they'd both died. He hadn't been able to return for the funeral and hadn't come back in the four years since. He at once felt both guilty and sad. He drained his mug and placed it on the bar. Joshua smiled.

"We'd better see about your room, hadn't we?" He motioned Nathan to follow him behind the bar and then led him into the rear of the pub. It was an old building, like most of the village and the passage was narrow, with low, small doorways. As they passed one of these doors, Joshua called out "We've a guest for dinner. Come out and meet 'im". As soon as the landlady emerged from the kitchen there was a flash of mutual recognition.

Nathan instantly remembered the buxom smiling woman and for one instant thought she was going to throw her arms around him, but all she did was take his hand in her own flour covered hands.

"Well, Nathan Holt, you've certainly grown up in these past few years," she said. Nathan felt himself colouring up a little, as he always did when a compliment came his way from a woman. "You've not changed much though. Your aunt Lily would have been proud of the way you've turned out. Dinner'll be ready in half an hour and you'll no doubt be hungry, so get yourself freshened up". Nathan smiled. Martha Carter sounded just like his aunt Lily. As she disappeared into the kitchen, Joshua took Nathan's arm.

"Your room's this way," he said. He led Nathan up a narrow, steep flight of stairs to an equally narrow landing, off which opened several doors. Joshua opened one and gestured for Nathan to enter. "This one's yours. If you want anything, just shout. We'll be sure to hear". He smiled and left Nathan alone in the small bedroom.

Tossing his kit-bag onto the bed, he looked at his new surroundings. There was a large bed, which almost filled the room, a small wooden chair, a wardrobe, a dressing table and a wash stand on which stood a bowl and a china jug filled with cold water. A small sash window let a little light into the room. Opening this, Nathan looked out over the backyard of the pub past some cottages and beyond to the fields of the surrounding countryside, the fields of his childhood. He could just make out the river that flowed near the village and then smiled as he suddenly remembered the time he'd fallen in that river when he'd been dared by his mates to cross the water on a fallen tree trunk. That had earned him more than just a good telling off from both his aunt and his uncle. Turning away from the window, he took off his jacket and washed his face. As he dried himself, he sighed with relief. He'd worried that coming back to his childhood home and seeing people who would still probably recognise him after ten years might be difficult and he was glad that the first trial was over. Whatever impulse had made him come back to Dalton Combe had been well worth following. He was feeling better already.

Chapter Two

Nathan was woken up by a light tapping on his door. Instantly awake, he jumped from the bed and winced as pain shot up his leg. Opening the bedroom door he found Joshua standing outside.

"Sorry to wake you lad," he said, "but dinner's on the table and Mrs. Carter says it'll spoil if you don't come down."

"I didn't realise I'd gone to sleep," Nathan said "but I'll be straight down." As Joshua turned and walked away, Nathan closed the door and pulled on his boots, which he didn't remember taking off, splashed some water on his face from the jug to wake himself up properly and replaced his jacket. Then he went downstairs to join Joshua and Martha at the table.

"No need to knock, just come on in," Martha called as he knocked lightly on the kitchen door. Joshua was already seated and a glorious smell of food swept over Nathan as he entered the room. He suddenly felt as if he had not eaten for days. He sat down at the table with Joshua and Martha placed a huge dish full of steaming hot stew in front of him, with two very large dumplings floating in it.

"Rabbit. One of my regulars brought 'im in, just the other day," Joshua mumbled through a mouthful of food, gesturing at the dish with his spoon and ignoring the glare he received from his wife. She sometimes despaired of his manners, much as she loved him. Nathan smiled back, his mouth already equally full, wondering idly how many free pints of beer would be drunk for that rabbit. Both men set about their food quickly and soon had empty dishes.

"I haven't tasted rabbit that well cooked since I lived with Aunt Lily," Nathan said and knew instinctively that he'd said the right thing from the smile that crossed Martha's face.

"She's a good cook is Martha," said Joshua, speaking as if his wife was in another room, and not sitting only three feet away from him. He wiped some grease from his chin. Then he grew more serious as if wondering how to say something. "What're you going to be doing now you're back, then?" he blurted out, ignoring another sharp look from Martha.

"Joshua Carter! You oughtn't to be asking such things," she said. "You should mind your own business."

"Mrs. Carter, I really don't mind," said Nathan, trying hard to suppress a laugh at the look on Joshua's face. He was not in the least crestfallen or dejected at what his wife obviously considered a social blunder.

"A little bit of rest for a while and after that, well, I'll see if there's any work going anywhere." It was not until that moment that Nathan had considered whether or not he'd be staying in Dalton Combe; the decision to come in the first place had surprised him. He had no plans of going elsewhere and no reason not to stay. "I'd have to find permanent lodgings, though," he said. "I hadn't really thought about it."

"You can stay here in the pub for as long as you want, Nathan," Martha said firmly, but before Nathan could argue with

16

her, Joshua spoke again.

"What kind of work did you have in mind?" asked Joshua. He quickly added "I might hear of something. To tell the truth, there's plenty of work on the farms – all the fit and healthy young men are in France." Before he had even realised what he had said, he was on the receiving end of another glare from his wife. There was an almost audible silence with Nathan sensing the older man's discomfort as the implication behind what he had just said dawned on him. "I didn't mean ... well, you know...," Joshua faltered and smiled.

"No, Joshua, that's where they all are and where I'd be if I hadn't copped for this." Nathan slapped his leg. No doubt Martha and Joshua were curious as to his wound, but there would be plenty of time to tell them. "Now, is there any farm in particular that needs men?"

"All of them," smiled Joshua, relieved. "Any farm in the district would be glad of help. I'll keep an ear to the ground." He relaxed visibly. Nathan smiled at Martha as if to reassure her that he was not upset by her husband's words and pushed his chair away from the table.

"Well, if you'll excuse me, I'll take a short walk. The doctors told me to keep exercising this leg or I'd gradually lose the use of it completely." he paused and then said to Martha "I thought I'd visit their graves," referring to his aunt and uncle. He'd paid the costs of their burial and of a headstone. She smiled and nodded her head in understanding. He turned to Joshua. "Is the cottage still there?"

17

"No, lad. There was little left standing of the place after the fire, and what there was wasn't safe. George Wilkins had it pulled down. Nothing has been rebuilt there." Nathan was not surprised. His uncle Joe had been a labourer for George Wilkins, living in a cottage tied to the farm, at a low rent.

"What happened that night? What caused the fire?" He'd often wondered.

"No one knows, Nathan." It was Martha who answered him. "I think if your aunt Lily could speak to us from above, she'd have something to say about your Uncle Joe's pipe. She was always on at him about it." Nathan smiled at the memory. He well remembered Aunt Lily's dislike of uncle Joe's pipe. It seemed a shame that it might have been the cause of their deaths.

Full to bursting from the meal, Nathan raised himself slowly from his chair and leaned over the table to Martha. "I can't remember when food tasted so good," he said with a smile and kissed her chastely on the cheek. "Thank you." He left the kitchen and made his way out to the market place, thinking to himself that no doubt poor Joshua Carter was now receiving a good telling off from his wife.

He emerged from the pub into the golden glow of the early evening sunlight and turned his footsteps towards the church and churchyard. The old church cast its shadow over part of it as he entered through the lych-gate and walked past the ancient yew trees towards the newer part of a graveyard that had been used by the village and its inhabitants for centuries.

The grave was simple, and like the rest of the churchyard,

well-tended, and Nathan stood looking at it for some minutes, with its simple inscription: 'Joseph Holt, born 1851, died 1912 and Lilian Marie Holt, born 1858, died 1912. Rest in everlasting sleep.' A feeling of deep sadness came over him. As accustomed as he thought he'd become to the idea of death, his aunt and uncle had been very close to him, more like the parents he had never known. He very much regretted not having been able to attend their funeral; this was his first chance to say goodbye. He turned away and as he walked back down the path, he passed the vicar heading towards the church door. The two men nodded in greeting, without speaking.

Dalton Combe seemed caught up in a magical spell of early evening peace as he turned into the lane which he thought led down to the river. The village appeared smaller than he remembered it, but he quickly realised that it was not Dalton Combe that had changed, but him. His outlook was wider and he'd experienced many things which had made him come to terms with himself. France had given him no choice. He shuddered at the thought of the War, but the feeling soon passed.

The village was too calm and too remote from the battlefields for such thoughts to linger. The cottages he walked past looked as they had done during his childhood and probably for long before that. The thick stone walls kept out the cold in winter and in summer kept the rooms cool. Each had a tidy little garden in front, making Nathan wonder how people found the time for growing flowers when there always seemed to be chores to finish and work to do. Many of the doors and windows were open, but he saw nobody, although the open doors reminded him of the sense of trust that everyone seemed to have. He remembered his aunt saying: 'There's nothing much worth stealing and anyway you've got to trust folks."

Nathan still had that trust, although it had been sorely tested at times in the army. His thoughts were interrupted as he stepped on a stone and his leg twisted awkwardly. Sweating with sudden pain, he leaned against a wall. Not for the first time, he wondered whether or not to find himself a strong stick for walking.

"Nice evenin' for a walk, ain't it?" said a voice. Nathan looked up abruptly. "Sorry, didn't mean to make you jump." The speaker was an elderly man who was looking at Nathan as if he felt he knew him. Patiently waiting by his side was a small terrier. Nathan found the man's look of partial recognition slightly unnerving, but knew it was something he'd become used to over the next few weeks.

"Oh, I was just thinking," said Nathan. "And yes, it is a nice evening for a walk, but there don't seem to be many people around".

"Working while they've got the light," the old man explained, obviously thinking Nathan should be aware of this basic fact of country life. He reached down and scratched his dog's ear. "Anyway, come on, Ben, we've got to be off. We're after rabbits," he explained to Nathan, who smiled. His uncle always used to say that when he was off to the pub for a pint, and guessed that's where the old man and his dog were off to now.

With his leg still throbbing, he watched the old man and his dog, perfect companions for each other, walking away up the lane and decided to walk on a little further himself.

When he reached the old stone bridge, he stopped and leaned on the parapet. Built over a narrow but shallow and fairly fast flowing part of the river, the bridge had replaced an old ford, but there was still quite a drop to the water below. The bridge was just wide enough to allow a horse and cart to cross, although numerous scratches testified to the times that farmers had not judged their position well enough.

Nathan was fascinated by the water bubbling under the bridge, flowing over the stones, and the light musical sounds it made were almost as enjoyable as watching the movement of the water. The only thing that spoiled the scene were the small groups of early evening midges flitting here and there.

Gazing absently down, Nathan suddenly laughed out loud and then anxiously looked around to see if anyone had heard him. He'd remembered how many times he'd looked over the side of this bridge as a boy and that he'd done nothing but reminisce like an old codger since coming back to the village. He decided to spend a few days re-acquainting himself with the countryside and to see all the places he remembered. This would probably be the best way of putting behind him all the things he'd rather not think about; the things he knew he'd never forget. When he grew tired of rambling, then would be the time to look for work.

Chapter Three

Smallbrook Farm, standing at the bottom of a hill topped with a copse, was, as its name suggested both not very large and sat on a stream, the same stream which further on in its course would run through nearby Dalton Combe. The farm buildings, a dairy and milking shed, a barn and a small farmhouse, were old, solid and in need of some repair. The yard around which these buildings were gathered was untidy and dotted with weeds. It opened out onto a meadow beyond which were two other fields belonging to the farm. The property was completed by an orchard and small flower and vegetable gardens.

It was still early enough in the morning for dew to be still lying on the grass, and for a fine dawn mist to be hanging in the air. The sun was bravely trying to break through, hinting of another fine day to come, when the farmhouse door opened and a young woman appeared. Jenny Tiley was a country girl of medium height, not too slim but not carrying any excess weight. Her long fair brown hair, her one vanity, was, both around the farm and around the village, worn tied back away from her face and generally covered with a headscarf. Once safely relaxed for the evening, she would let it fall loosely about her shoulders. Her face had a country-woman's complexion, alive with a healthy glow and wore, for the most part, a friendly welcoming expression. Jenny would not have considered herself an attractive woman, but a smile from her had been known to make many a village man wish he were a few years younger.

She was carrying a large bowl which she carefully placed on a fence before opening the gates of two small pens. A cacophony of geese, hens and ducks emerged, crowding round her as she took up the bowl and scattered grain on the ground for them, which they attacked hungrily. Returning the empty bowl to the farmhouse, she re-emerged moments later, heading towards the meadow, where her small herd of just five cows had already gathered at the gate. As she opened it, the cows moved towards her then past her into the farmyard, responding to her gentle calls. Udders hung heavy with milk, each cow moved without hesitation towards the milking shed, much to the annoyance of the feeding birds, which fluttered angrily out of the way. The young woman tethered each cow in its place and they all began eating, munching contentedly on hay from the rack in front of them.

Tightening a scarf around her hair and picking up a small three legged stool and a pail, she bent to the task of milking her small herd, her head pressed into the flank of the cow as she squirted milk into the pail, 'pull and squeeze' the mantra going through her mind. Finishing with the last one, she turned them all loose into the meadow once more and returned to the milking shed where she covered the small churns into which she had tipped each full pail of milk. Then it was time for breakfast, after one final chore of ushering the geese into the orchard where they would spend their day eating grass.

She returned to the house, humming softly to herself as she crossed the yard and went into the farmhouse kitchen. In the sparsely furnished room, there was a large table which she had to walk around to get to an equally large dresser with an assortment of plates and cups. The floor was covered with stone flags, well worn near the door and sink, where over the years countless feet had walked on them. The young woman, having picked up a cup, now walked across to the range and placed a kettle over the fire. She made herself a cup of tea and sank into a chair by the huge kitchen table.

Since her husband had gone to France, it had been hard work on the farm, small though it was. A man did come in to help her with the heavier work, but mostly she was on her own. The worst thing was the loneliness. She still found it difficult to believe that the man she loved was dead, killed in the mud of France. Unwanted, the memory of when she'd been told came to mind.

She'd been out in the farmyard, feeding the birds, when she heard the tinkle of a bell and saw the postmaster's son cycle into the yard. Putting the corn bowl on a wall out of reach, she'd waited for him, feeling nervous.

"Hello Johnny. You don't often come out here," she said to the lad.

"It's an errand for dad, Mrs. Tiley," he said breathlessly. I've got this for you," he continued, handing over a telegram for her. He knew as well as she did what it was likely to contain and his young face showed discomfort as well as sadness. He turned away to return to the village.

"No, wait", the young woman said with a friendly smile and asked him if he would like a glass of ginger beer before cycling back. To her relief, he'd said no and cycled away, with one quick glance back at her standing in the farmyard staring at the unopened envelope, her smile gone. It stayed unopened until she'd retreated to the kitchen. She spent the following hours simply staring at the bland impersonal official message that said her husband had been "killed in action"

Sitting now, at that same table, Jenny Tiley reflected on the desolate loss she'd felt at that time, a feeling that often returned in the deepest parts of the night. Even while reading the telegram, though, she'd decided that she wasn't going to leave the farm. It was her husband's dream and she would work as hard as she could to keep that dream alive. In the end, it had become her dream. Now, eighteen months later, she was tired but proud of what she'd done.

Her thoughts were interrupted by a loud clucking. With the kitchen door open, some hopeful and adventurous chickens had wandered in from the yard. She shooed them back out and sat down to plan her day's work. Butter for the village shop was her first priority; the shopkeeper, Mr Williams was quite happy to sell it for her, along with any spare eggs she might have. Any surplus milk she sold to Mr. Wilkins, her landlord, who deducted the cash from her rent.

Crossing the yard to the milking shed, she picked up one of the small churns she had filled with milk earlier and half-dragging, half carrying it, went through to the small room she liked to think of as her dairy. It was spotless; in one corner stood a butter churn, into which she managed to tip the milk. Shutting the hatch, she began to turn the handle, hearing the fresh milk slop around. After a while, her arm started to ache as it usually did and the handle became harder to turn. She stopped, poured the buttermilk into a bowl and took out the cream which had been separated by the churning. She poured that into another bowl and began to beat it with a large wooden spoon. Slowly, small grains appeared in the liquid. She hurried across the room and took a large strainer and a piece of muslin from a cupboard. She put the muslin in the strainer and carefully poured the butter grains and remaining milk into the muslin. Then she poured in cold water to wash away the milk.

Carrying the muslin across to a well-scrubbed table, Jenny tipped the solid lump of butter out. The next step was to beat the butter until there was no water left and then shape it into small blocks. On some mornings, she amused herself by making all sorts of shapes, but this particular morning, she restrained herself and got on with the work. She carried on with this all morning, with one butter churn of milk after another, until by lunchtime, she had a fair number of blocks of set butter, all wrapped individually in greased paper. Then she made herself some lunch.

After eating, she loaded the basket on the front of her bicycle with both eggs and butter and tied a gaily coloured cloth over the top. Then she set off for the village. She loved cycling through the countryside, it made her feel such a part of it. It was this joy of being part of the countryside that she'd shared with her husband, both of them having been brought up on farms. People had advised the young couple not to take on the responsibility of becoming tenant farmers, but Edward had wanted to do it. It was a step up the social ladder, he insisted, something that was important to him, if not to her. Both Smallbrook Farm and the village had entranced them on their first visit and despite the almost never ending hard work, now she couldn't imagine herself living any other kind of life.

As Jenny neared the narrow bridge into the village, she saw a horse and cart coming the other way. She stopped and dismounted from her bicycle, intending to wait for it to cross. She recognised the driver, Harry Mason, who came to help her out at Smallbrook, and waited with childlike anticipation. Harry wasn't renowned for his abilities in crossing the narrow bridge, becoming stuck so often that children from the village would often gather round and wait if they knew he was coming. Although he didn't have an audience, he didn't let her down, for he noticed her and waved just as he began to cross the bridge, and the cart inevitably jammed where he hadn't lined it up properly.

'Bloody bridge!" he exclaimed, then remembered her standing there and looked up guiltily. She politely pretended not to have heard and he carried on swearing under his breath. Then he sighed, took off his jacket and climbed down. He unhitched the horse and walked it over to Jenny.

"Mrs. Tiley, Would you 'old her for me?" Suppressing a smile, she took the reins and watched as he re-crossed the bridge and bent to pushing the cart into position to get it over the bridge. Before either of them had really noticed his presence, a young man, also in his shirtsleeves, had joined him. Between them they quickly had the cart not only freed but also over the bridge. The new arrival was a stranger to Jenny, but she smiled a hello when he looked at her as he walked past out of the village carrying his jacket. She caught a glimpse of a friendly face but with a strange far-away look. Harry, re-harnessing the horse, saw her watch the man walk away.

"Strange, that young man..."

"What?" she asked as Harry broke in on her thoughts. "Oh, yes. He didn't even say hello. Do you know who he is?"

"Oh yes. His name's Nathan Holt. He's staying at the pub. Got hurt in France, so I heard and invalided out of the Army or something. Used to live in the village with his aunt and uncle, them as was killed in the cottage fire. Still, I got to be off. Bye, Mrs. Tiley." Jenny waved and pushed her bicycle on into the village, in the opposite direction to that taken by the young man.

By the time she was leaning her bicycle against a wall in the village, Nathan Holt was no longer on her mind. She went into the small shop, where another customer was being served. Despite the familiarity of the shop, Jenny as always, had time to have a good look around. Behind the counter were big jars containing sweets, kept well out of reach of little fingers and below these were the large sacks of things like flour and sugar from which Mr. Williams the grocer weighed out people's purchases on a pair of massive scales with brass weights. The shop, whenever she was in it, seemed to be a cacophony of noise. Along with customer's voices, there would be the clatter of the scales and the tinkling of the bell over the door as people came and went.

"More butter for me, Mrs. Tiley?" the grocer asked as his last customer left.

"Yes, and eggs, in the basket on my bicycle," she replied.

29

"If you want them, that is," she added. She was always nervously grateful of his kindness in buying her produce from her, taking nothing for granted.

"Oh I certainly do," Mr. Williams said, smiling. There was quite a demand for her butter in the village. There was an indefinable taste which appealed to people, and of course Jenny was not about to part with the recipe. "You wait there, and I'll just fetch it," he added opening the shop door to an accompanying tinkle from the bell. "How much is there?" he asked when he came back clutching the parcel.

"Only about eight pounds, I think," she replied.

"I'll weigh it and see," said the grocer preparing his scales. After a little clattering, he looked at her and smiled. "Nine-and-a-half pounds. You nearly gave some away again." Jenny smiled back, thinking that in future she must really weigh it before bringing it to the village. "Now, how much did we agree on? Eightpence a pound wasn't it?"

"No, Mr Williams, it was not. It was sevenpence a pound, as you well know," she added, laughing. The old grocer actually blushed. No matter how well meant or touching his generosity, she could never accept it. "Eightpence a pound is what you sell it for." He nodded and took some money from his till for her. Smiling even more broadly, he asked "Is there anything I can get for you while you're here?"

"No, not today, thank you, Mr. Williams," she replied. The grocer watched her as she walked out of the door. Like many people in the village he admired her courage in battling on with the farm and making a success of it. The close-knit community of the village had shared her grief over the loss of her husband and she was one of the few people in the village with whom the normally chatty grocer didn't discuss the War. Mrs. Thompson, who'd lost two sons as early as September 1914, was another.

Outside in the sunshine, Jenny was unaware of the grocer's thoughts, but for some reason suddenly thought about the War herself and a chill ran through her. She shook the thoughts away and mounting her bicycle, began the ride back to Smallbrook.

Chapter Four

The scene was one common across the English countryside for centuries, a man leading a horse and cart across the fields on a bright sunny morning. The man, John Evans, a farmhand at Home Farm, was walking slowly alongside a huge gentle shire horse, which was pulling a cart. The muscles of the horse still rippled powerfully under its tan skin in spite of its age. Evans sighed deeply and then coughed, the start of a coughing fit which reached his chest and cut off his breath. He called to the horse to stop and sat on the grass to rest and get his breath.

"I reckon that you and me are both of us past our best," he said to the horse, which just gazed at him in return. The coughing fits were becoming more frequent although the fresh country air was helping the old man.

Horses were his life; he'd worked with them when he started in the coal pits of South Wales at the age of ten, as a stable boy. The coalfields of the Swansea Valley used a lot of ponies for hauling coal trucks underground and his job had been to look after the poor animals that so rarely saw the sun, to feed them and care for them. Then, after a few years, he'd reluctantly moved on to much more physical and better paid work at the coal-face and had lost contact with the ponies he'd come to love. Later, with thirty years of coal dust in his lungs, he'd gone full circle and found himself back in the stables. Now, here he was, in the open air, working with horses on the land, the fulfillment of a life's dream. He coughed again and not for the first time, saw blood in his phlegm. It's only a matter of time for both of us, he thought sadly, looking at the old horse.

Evans' life had changed drastically in 1914, some six months before the war had started. His son, a miner in the same colliery as John, had given up his mining job and moved to Devon, to try his hand at driving wagons in a haulage business and had persuaded his widowed father to move with him. The whole family, father, son, daughter-in-law and three children had moved from the Welsh valleys to the Devon countryside. A cottage went with the job, and the family soon settled in. Then the outbreak of war changed their lives, just as it changed the lives of countless others.

Evans' son, in a fit of patriotic fervour, like so many other young men, had volunteered for the British Expeditionary Force, to help defend what was being called "brave little Belgium" against the German hordes. It fell upon Evans to look after the family. The haulage company insisted the family move out of the cottage and Evans had begun to help out on a local farm with odd jobs, and had then found work that came with a cottage in Dalton Combe provided by George Wilkins, the farmer.

His experience with horses had stood him in good stead; with many of the men away, farm workers were scarce. He'd suddenly found himself in demand. Naturally, all of the horses he worked with were old - the British Army's expenditure of horses had been quite horrific in the early part of the War and most of the fit and healthy animals had been taken - and should have been put out to pasture.

Evans lit his pipe, filling it with his favourite 'black shag' tobacco and ignoring the mine doctor's words which echoed in his ears every time he took a puff, "If you'll take my advice, you'll give up that pipe of yours." That was a joke thought Evans. I spent years underground chipping away at coal with a pick in the semi darkness breathing in coal dust and the mine doctor wanted him to give up his pipe. He laughed at the memory, a laugh which quickly turned into another cough. This brought tears to his eyes, which he wiped away with his sleeve.

"It's been over ten years since that doctor told me to give you up," he said to his pipe, "and I think maybe it's about time I did." He put it out and slipped it back into his pocket. Then he made himself more comfortable and beginning to get his breath back, relaxed for a few moments.

Nathan saw the old man sitting by the cart as he walked up the narrow lane and decided to go over for a chat. He'd seen nobody that morning except Joshua and his wife, and felt in need of some company. He went through the gate and walked across the field. The old man seemed to have fallen asleep. Nathan coughed gently as he reached him.

"Good morning," he said.

"Eh? What?" said the old man, struggling to come to his senses.

"I said good morning," said Nathan, a big smile on his face.

"And a good morning to you," said Evans, now fully awake. He stood up slowly and started coughing. "Nothing...to...worry about," he said to Nathan between coughs, noticing the young man's concerned look. The coughing passed off quickly. "Just a

35

present I had for working in the pits. Don't know of any of the lads I worked with who aren't already dead or suffering like me. But it's too nice a day for such talk. John Evans is the name," he said, holding out his hand.

"Nathan Holt," came the reply as Nathan gripped the outstretched hand firmly. "Could you do with some company?"

"That I could, Nathan Holt," said Evans with a smile. "Always nice to have someone to talk to." The two men began to walk, and Evans, a natural talker, told Nathan all about himself and his life, especially his working life in the colliery. Nathan found it unbelievable that men could work in such conditions, and found his mind drifting back to the trenches in France. Eventually Evans told Nathan that his own son was out in France. "He's on the Somme somewhere, God help him. We don't hear from him often, but he seems alright." Evans noticed the cloud that passed over Nathan's face. "You were on the Somme, too, were you?". Nathan nodded.

"It's something I've lived through, which is a lot more than many other men," said Nathan. "But I really don't know if I can ever live with what I've done and seen." Evans said nothing, waiting for the younger man to continue, while the only sound was the singing of the birds in the hedgerows. "Your son is on the Somme, you say?" It was Evans' turn to nod. "It's not a nice place to be – I'm glad I'm out of it. There's nothing but mud, miles of stinking trenches, barbed wire and rats. God knows what the French will do with it when the war ends. It's an absolute wilderness. I've seen men out there give themselves a Blighty rather than try to stick it out any longer." He noticed a puzzled look on Evans' face. " A Blighty is a wound that gets you sent back to England," he explained. One bloke in my platoon shot his foot off with his Lee Enfield, saying 'I'd rather be a cripple than a corpse'."

"What happened to him?" Evans asked.

"Our lieutenant saw him do it. The military police came for him. He was shot in front of a firing squad as an example as soon as he could stand up. It's funny, but men will run the risk of a firing squad rather than stand up in front of Hun machine guns. Either way really, it's like killing yourself." Nathan sounded bitter.

"It sounds like hell," said Evans.

"It is. I'm glad I'm back here. It's hard to believe that it's going on while we're talking."

"What happened to get you sent back?" asked Evans. Nathan paused before answering. He had tried hard not to think about when he had actually got wounded. "If you'd rather not talk about it...," continued Evans.

"No, it's alright. It happened on a night patrol in no-man's land. I was one of the lucky ones. We got through our wire and were going across the mud towards the Hun minefields when a flare went up. Just a routine flare - but one of ours. Some silly bugger in one of the other trenches had thought he'd seen someone moving about, so he thought he'd check it. Anyway the Hun machine guns opened up on us, and like I said, I was lucky - when the bullets cut into my legs I was thrown into a shell hole. That saved my life. The other two poor sods were cut to pieces. I was stuck in that hole for nearly two days until they could get someone to fetch me in." Nathan was completely oblivious to the countryside around him. He was back in the shell hole, half-delirious with pain, waiting in the pouring rain to be carried back to his trench, but almost convinced that no-one would come for him. The fear that had gripped him then, the fear of dying alone, with his blood slowly trickling from his body, now gripped him again.

"Here boyo, are you alright?" The lilting Welsh voice broke in on his thoughts. "Are you alright lad? You've gone white."

"Alright? Yes I'm fine," said Nathan, slowly coming to his senses again.

"Look, we'd better stop here for a few minutes. I'm in no hurry. Whoa," Evans called out to the horse, which stopped immediately without any further encouragement, as if grateful for the rest. "Come on, sit you down, and have a drop of this. He pulled a small flask from a jacket pocket. "Handed down from me Da this flask was. I try to use it as much as I can."

"What's in it?" asked Nathan, taking the flask from the Welshman's outstretched hand.

"A drop o' rum. It'll warm the cockles of your heart will that." Nathan had to agree as the fiery liquid burnt his throat, finally leaving him with a pleasant warm feeling in his stomach.

"Thank you," he said, passing the flask back. "That's nice rum, not like the rough stuff we sometimes managed to get hold of in the trenches."

"That's enough talk of trenches and war, my lad. It's a grand day, and we're going to enjoy it." Evans had been shocked

38

by the change in the young man's appearance while he talked and was now determined to keep his mind away from what seemed a difficult subject. "Will you walk a little further with me?" he asked. "It's good to have some company, and he doesn't talk much." Evans said gesturing at the horse. Nathan said he would, laughing, and they continued slowly, the old horse pulling the cart steadily now that they had reached the top of the ridge and had pulled out onto a different lane. "It's a fine view," continued Evans.

"It is," agreed Nathan. From where they were walking, they had a view over the entire vale, with the village at one end - Nathan could make out the road on which he'd entered the village on the other side of the valley, weaving its way through the trees, and the gentle leveling out of the hills on either side into the lower land that lay between the vale and the sea. Even from this height, Nathan knew without looking that the sea was still too far away to be seen. Looking once more at the village, he then looked down the length of the vale, following the road across the narrow pack-horse bridge and through the woods towards the Wilkins farm, the biggest farm in the area. Mr and Mrs Wilkins had lived at Manor Farm for nearly forty years, and before that, Mr Wilkins' father had run the place. They were the nearest thing to local gentry that the village possessed, but even they were a long way removed from what was normally regarded as the 'upper classes'. Nathan remembered George Wilkins as an angry man, best avoided by the village boys.

Enjoying the view, Nathan looked again along the road, back towards the village and noticed for the first time the old weather beaten stone farmhouse just below what he knew as the

Bluebell Wood. When he was a boy in the village, the house had been deserted, and the village boys had always played there; now, to his surprise, there was smoke coming from the chimneys and chickens and ducks in the farmyard.

"Who lives down there now?" he asked the old Welshman. "The place was empty when I was a boy."

"What, Smallbrook? There's been a young couple name of Tiley there since I moved here. The poor lass has been on her own since losing her husband in France. Last year I think it was."

Chapter Five

The two men, the old Welshman and the young soldier, continued slowly up the lane in a companionable silence, broken only by increasingly more frequent coughs from John Evans, whose breathing seemed to Nathan to be a little laboured. He put his hand on the older man's arm and stopped him in a shady spot.

"Why don't you climb up on the cart, and I'll lead the horse," Nathan said. "Get yourself a bit of a rest, and get that cough sorted out." Evans was now leaning on the cart, his face red, almost gasping for breath.

"No," he said between coughs. "I'll be fine." A little blood had appeared on his lips and he dabbed it away with a handkerchief already dotted with dark spots. "'Ave to keep this away from my daughter-in-law," he spluttered, waving the cloth and trying to smile. Despite Evans' attempt at joking, Nathan was very concerned about the old Welshman. Coughing up blood was never a good sign, no matter how little there might be. Evans took another drink from his flask and to Nathan's consternation, caught his breath and collapsed to the ground coughing and spluttering. The still un-stopped flask fell from his hand and rolled beneath the cart, leaking its contents into the dirt.

Nathan fell to his knees beside the sick man, relieved to see he was still breathing, if a little erratically. He pulled him into a sitting position, leaning against a wheel of the cart and retrieved the flask, slipping it into the Welshman's waistcoat pocket. Then he sat down himself and waited for a wave of pain in his own leg to pass. It was obvious to Nathan that Evans had to see a doctor, and as soon as possible. He stood up and placing his hands under the older man's armpits, pulled him upright with little effort and only a slight groan from Evans, who remained unconscious.

Nathan had already met the doctor in the village, a Doctor Allerby, a man who seemed to know what he was talking about, inspired confidence and had spent some time talking to Nathan about not becoming too reliant on pain killers, but to concentrate on strengthening his leg. They had also talked about Nathan's nightmares, for which he'd prescribed a sleeping draught. Evans would almost certainly be one of his patients, so the doctor should be aware of his condition.

Having already found that the old man weighed very little, Nathan had no trouble lifting him into the back of the cart. Evans remained unconscious, but once lying down, his breathing seemed a little easier, to Nathan's relief. There was nothing in the back of the cart to make the Welshman any more comfortable, so Nathan slipped off his jacket, rolled it up and used it to provide a pillow. When he was as sure that Evans was as comfortable and secure as possible, he turned the horse around and started down the lane to the village, hurrying as much as he could, but always aware of Evans' comfort.

The doctor's house, was, perhaps befitting his importance to the community, one of the larger houses in the village, situated just away from the Market Place, but still easily accessible to the villagers. Walking along the short path, his eyes were drawn to the net curtained window to the left of the door, where he knew Doctor Allerby had his office, and wondered if he had a patient with him. He also found himself praying that the doctor had not been called out anywhere. To Nathan's relief, the doctor himself answered the knock on his door. He was obviously surprised to see Nathan standing there, but quickly took in what Nathan was saying about John Evans.

"Another attack, eh?" he said almost to himself. And then said to Nathan "I'll get my bag," disappearing back into the house. He quickly returned and followed Nathan down the path to the roadway. When they reached the cart, Evans seemed worse again to Nathan. Allerby quickly noticed that the floor of the cart was speckled with spots of blood from his coughing. He sat the sick man up and produced a small bottle from his bag which he held it to the old Welshman's lips. Tasting it, Evans drank a little more. Satisfied that his patient had taken enough, Doctor Allerby took the bottle away and watched as the coughing and gasping slowly eased and John Evans himself relaxed. Then, without any warning, the sick man was sound asleep. Allerby smiled at Nathan. "Come on, we'd better get him home," he said. When Nathan looked a little puzzled, as he had no idea where Evans lived, the doctor said "I'm a fairly frequent visitor. I know where to take him."

John Evans, like most of the villagers, lived in a tied cottage and as they stopped in front of it, the doctor continued, "We'll have to carry him in," but was surprised by Nathan's reply.

"No, I can manage. You'd better warn them he's coming." As Allerby knocked on the door of the cottage, he again picked

43

the old man up easily and carried him through the now open door and into the main living room. He was met by a worried-looking middle-aged woman in animated conversation with Doctor Allerby. "Where shall I put him?" he asked.

"Come with me. I'll show you," the woman said. Nathan took her to be Evans daughter-in-law and was not surprised by the musical Welsh lilt to her voice. The doctor followed them up the stairs and into a small bedroom, where Nathan carefully laid the old man on the bed. As he turned to go back downstairs, he heard the doctor say

"I've given him some laudanum, Mary. He'll sleep for a while now. Leave him in his clothes and don't disturb him." Then the two of them followed Nathan downstairs and back into the living room. The small cottage reminded Nathan of his aunt and uncle's home, but before his memories had a chance to flood back, Mary Evans interrupted them, speaking to the doctor. "I'll be settling up on Saturday when Da gets his money?" she asked. Nathan noticed a concerned look on her face and, as he turned away, a half smile on the doctor's face.

"Well, Mrs. Evans, my wife has always been partial to your home made pickles," he began. The woman scurried off to the kitchen and returned with a number of jars which she thrust into Doctor Allerby's arms. It was noticeable that some of the concern had passed from her face.

"It'll be a nice cup of tea you'll both be wanting?" she asked. Doctor Allerby declined, while Nathan gratefully and readily accepted. Saying his farewells, the doctor departed and Nathan followed Mrs. Evans through to the small kitchen. Within

44

minutes he was holding a steaming cup of tea while Mrs Evans was piling sugar into it.

"He's a kind man, Doctor Allerby," the older woman said. Nathan agreed. He'd been thinking the same thing. He'd heard that country doctors quite often accepted payment other than money, but this was the first time he'd come across it himself. Somehow it made Doctor Allerby seem even more likeable.

"Will you have some cake?" she asked. Again, Nathan readily accepted and almost as soon as he'd taken his first bite, he was asked another question. "How is it you were with Da this morning?" Struggling not to speak with his mouth full of cake, Nathan explained how they met while he was out walking. "This is the worst he's been you know. A very ill man is Da." She looked sad. "Mr." she began and hesitated. "I don't know your name," she said.

"Holt," he replied.

"Well, Mr. Holt, thank you for what you've done. It would have been bad for Da if you hadn't happened to be there." Nathan smiled and began to say that he'd only done what anyone would have done, but she hushed him and urged him to eat his cake, which he was finding delicious. He could tell something was on her mind. "It's wrong of me to impose on you further when you've been so kind, Mr. Holt, but I can't leave Da here on his own, and our Jack's not back, and Mr. Wilkins will be wanting his horse back. Could you take it up to him for me? I'd be happy to give you something for your trouble," she added. Wondering idly how she would manage that, and not really fond of pickles, Nathan said he would quite happily return the horse.

45

"But I don't want anything for doing it," he added with a smile. Finishing his tea and cake he started towards the front door, then turned towards her. "If there's anything I can do while Mr. Evans is ill, I'm staying at The Lamb. Just send a message."

"You're a kind man, Mr. Holt," she said, gripping his arm. She followed him to the front door and watched him lead the horse and cart away.

Chapter Six

After unharnessing him from the cart, Nathan tied the old horse to a ring in the stable wall and began to brush him down with firm downward strokes with a brush from the stable. The horse seemed to enjoy the treatment and Nathan wondered idly how often it was done. Earlier that afternoon he'd led the horse into the farmyard after leaving John Evans with his daughter-in-law. Mr. Wilkins, Evans' employer had seen him and come rushing across. Nathan recognised him immediately. The well-built, red-faced farmer had not changed at all while Nathan had been away.

"What's up? Where's old John Evans?" he'd demanded without even as much as a greeting. "And why have you got one of my horses?" George Wilkins was a hard man and didn't tolerate fools. He was also inclined to initially be aggressive towards people. Generally disliked in the area by people who didn't care to get to know him any better, he kept himself to himself and liked it that way.

"He was taken bad up on the hill where he was re-building one of your walls," Nathan replied shortly, aggrieved by the man's tone. "I happened to be with him, and made sure he got home". He paused, looking the older farmer straight in the eye. "And I've got your horse because I thought it was best to return him to you and because Mary Evans asked me to." George Wilkins had eyed Nathan up carefully while he was speaking, and a big grin had spread over his face.

"Well lad, it's much appreciated," he said. Nathan had been surprised by what seemed to be an abrupt change of mood, and unsettled that he'd misjudged the man simply on what he had heard about him rather than forming his own opinions. "You say you took John home? What happened?" Wilkins sounded anxious, which again didn't fit with what Nathan had heard about him. Nathan then explained how he happened to be with the old Welshman.

"It's good that you were there, lad. John's getting on a bit, but he's a good worker. It was his chest again then?" Nathan nodded. "He was a coal-miner, you know. That's where he picked up his bad chest. Can't say that I'd like to work underground away from the sun."

"He told me. It can't be much of a life," Nathan agreed. The thought of being underground brought back disagreeable memories of trench dugouts in France. Mr. Wilkins interrupted his thoughts, asking

"How long will I be without old John, lad? Do you know, or do I need to ask the doctor?"

"The doctor said a week, maybe two."

"That means some jobs will have to wait - I've got no one to spare," the farmer mused to himself. Nathan smiled, then impetuously said

"You'll be short-handed while Mr Evans is sick?"

"That I will," said Mr Wilkins.

"Well I've nothing to do but walk around - I'll fill in for him as well as I can, if you could use the help." The farmer, who had taken a liking to the young man, smiled and nodded.

"I could, lad and I'd certainly be glad of it,"

"There is one thing, Mr. Wilkins," Nathan began and the farmer's warm smile faded a little. "I don't need the money, so I'd be glad if you could see that Mr Evans still got his full week's pay." Nathan glanced at Mr Wilkins to how this had been received. The farmer's smile had returned.

"Don't worry about old John, lad, we'll make sure he's got a bit of food on his table as well, and the neighbours will rally around. What's important to me is that the work's done, not where the money goes, but I'm sure John and his family will be grateful to you for your offer." He put his hand on Nathan's shoulder. "Here we are, with me just having taken you on and I don't know your name. What do they call you?"

"Nathan Holt." The farmer looked thoughtful.

"The young rascal that lived with Joe and Lily?" Nathan nodded. "Joe was always talking about you and how much Lily liked getting your letters." He put his hand on Nathan's shoulder. "Sad business, that," he said. Then he shrugged a little. "Still, if you're as good a worker as your uncle was..."

That had been some hours earlier and Nathan had almost immediately been sent off to repair a broken gate. It was after finishing that job that he'd returned to the stable with the old horse. He paused in his work and cleared the brush with the curry-comb. He straightened up and even standing to his full height he only came to the horse's shoulder. He soon finished the chore and leaving the stable, crossed the yard to the farmhouse, where he knocked on the kitchen door.

˜Come on in, the door's open," Mr. Wilkins called. As Nathan entered, he saw the old farmer sitting at a wooden table, a mug of cider in his hand. "Will you have one?" Wilkins asked, gesturing at a jug.

"I will," Nathan replied, "it's been a hot day." The older man stood up and fetched another pewter mug from the kitchen dresser.

"Help yourself," he said as he passed it to Nathan, gesturing again at the jug. There's plenty there - we make our own." Many farmers did make their own ciders, and even in the same district, tastes could vary wildly. Nathan poured himself a full mug and accepted Mr. Wilkins gestured offer to sit down. "Is there something you want?" the older man asked directly.

"No, just to tell you I've finished the gate and put Captain back in the stable. Is there anything else you want me to do today?" The farmer shook his head.

"Not that can be started today, but I've got things that need doing tomorrow. When you've finished your cider, get yourself back off to the Lamb. Martha's a good cook. You wouldn't want to miss out on one of her meals and if she's saved it for you and it spoils, you'll be in real trouble." The two chatted sociably until Nathan's mug was empty and by the time he stood to leave, Nathan knew that George Wilkins was misunderstood only because he wanted to keep himself to himself. They shook hands and Nathan walked out into the farmyard.

He was deep in thought as he strolled along the lane towards the village. The latter days of spring were still in full bloom and not yet quite ready to burst into the hot days of summer, with the natural abundance of fruit that came with it. The changing of the seasons was such an important part of English country life, and Nathan, like everyone else had his favourite. For him, it was that far-off autumn when the blackberry bushes hung heavy with the ripe dark purplish fruit. Nathan clearly remembered brambling, as his aunt used to call it. Each day would bring more scratches, the payment for full baskets of plump blackberries his aunt would turn into delicious pies and jam. The taste of that jam - he could still bring it to mind - was one of the best tastes he'd ever experienced.

Nathan slipped all too easily into a vaguely melancholic mood and remembered another chore he'd been expected to do, collecting elderberries. His aunt used them for wine, as did many country people, a wine he was rarely allowed to taste and then never by his aunt, only his uncle. It was always used hot whenever he had a cold. He was still deep in his memories when he reached the Lamb and climbed the stairs, reaching his room without seeing anybody.

Chapter Seven

"So you've found yourself some work, then," Joshua said some time later when they were sitting in the kitchen having their evening meal. As usual the kitchen door was open for him to hear if any customers came in. Being a publican wasn't a good life, Nathan thought. Sunday was Joshua's only real day of rest, when the pub was only open for a few hours at lunchtime and then again in the evening. Even so, he'd been amazed when Joshua told him that on a Sunday, when the pub was closed, anyone who had walked more than three miles had the right to one drink. Something to do with ancients rights, he'd said. With licensing hours from half past six in the morning until eleven o'clock at night, Joshua largely pleased himself during the week. "Old man Wilkins fancies 'imself as Squire, you know," said Joshua.

"Squire? What happened to the Hardings?" Nathan asked.

"They both died the year after you left. The old house has been empty since then," Joshua said.

"Such a shame about the house," said Martha. "It's a lovely old place." There was a break in the conversation while they ate.

Nathan had told Joshua and Martha what had happened during the day. Martha had immediately worried about how John Evans' daughter-in-law would cope and rushed off to see her after their meal.

"I've only got a job until John Evans is up and about again,"

Nathan replied.

"He's not a well man at the best of times," Joshua said, "but he's a tough 'un and he likes a pint, does that old Welshman. George Wilkins is likely to want to hang on to you for a while, you know. There's not many strong young men around here these days." Nathan had been thinking the same thing himself that afternoon as he'd worked on the gate. He wanted something to do something to keep him occupied and busy. He said as much to Joshua. "Have you thought of going back to Exeter?" the landlord asked.

"And end up in a factory, Joshua? I've not got what it takes for an office job and besides, I don't want to be stuck inside all day."

"Well, you're welcome here as long as you want to stay, you know that" was Joshua's only reply.

Nathan was at Home Farm early next day and waited at the stables for Mr. Wilkins, to appear. Strolling across the farmyard, George Wilkins was already rolling up his shirtsleeves readying himself for work.

"Mornin', Nathan," he bellowed from some distance away.

"Morning, Mr. Wilkins," Nathan replied when the farmer was closer. "What was it you wanted me to do today?"

"Not so fast. I expect you could down a cup of tea first?" Nathan nodded. A cup of tea was always welcome. The two men re-crossed the yard and went into the kitchen. Mrs. Wilkins, a large homely woman, wearing a full length flowery apron which could have been the twin of that worn by Martha at the pub, was busily clearing up the breakfast dishes. "Have you emptied that pot yet, Alice?" George asked.

"No, I haven't. I had a feeling you'd be wanting another," she answered without turning from the sink. She paused as she turned and noticed Nathan. "The tea's for you is it, young man?" Without waiting for him to reply, she began to fill two large mugs. "Mr. Wilkins here has already drunk enough this morning to float a Dreadnought in," she continued, with a warm smile. She guided Nathan towards the table. "Have you had breakfast?" she suddenly asked.

"Of course he's had breakfast. He's staying at The Lamb. Martha Carter wouldn't let him out without feeding him," George Wilkins interrupted.

"Well, actually...," Nathan began.

"You haven't, have you?" Mrs. Wilkins said, eyebrows raised. Nathan explained that he had slipped out without Martha noticing. "Well, bacon and eggs it is, then. You can't be expected to work on an empty stomach," was the decisive reply, with a meaningful glance at her husband as if inviting him to argue with her.

"Just a bacon sandwich would be fine, Mrs. Wilkins," said Nathan.

"Make that two," added the farmer. He then went on to ask Nathan about France. Nathan explained about the conditions in the trenches while they ate. The farmer's wife was shocked. "We don't know what's really going on," George Wilkins said. "Only what's in the papers and you can't really believe them." Nathan agreed. From the things he'd seen in newspapers since his return, he knew how much they distorted or hid the truth. It was almost a glorification of horror. George Wilkins returned to the subject of their day. "There are some dead trees that need moving up in Harden's Copse. Are you up to it?" Nathan nodded, knowing the older man was referring to his leg.

"Will you want lunch to take with you?" Alice Wilkins asked.

"No, send one of the boys up later and make sure 'e brings a good drop of cider," George laughed.

"I'll send young Jack Evans," Alice said decisively. "He'll enjoy being up there with you and might even be able to help a bit." George nodded. He'd asked John Evans' daughter in law to send her eldest son up to the farm.

"Ready then, lad?" Nathan nodded, unable to speak through his last mouthful of bacon sandwich. Swallowing quickly, he thanked Alice Wilkins for the food and followed her husband out into the yard.

Within half an hour of harnessing Captain to the cart and making a selection of saws and axes, Mr. Wilkins and Nathan were in the Copse. It was composed almost completely of beech trees, with little undergrowth. With the day beginning to warm up, they were both glad of the shade the canopy of leaves offered.

"We'll start on the far side," said the farmer. "That's where most of the fallen wood is." They walked soundlessly through the wood and came out on the edge of a hill. They began work and were soon soaked with sweat from their exertions. The fallen trees and branches were cut up into logs and stacked carefully on the ground: it would take a number of trips to get them all back to the farm. It was with some surprise that they both heard a young boy's voice calling for them.

"Over 'ere, Jack, there's a good lad," George Wilkins bellowed. "That'll be our lunch, Nathan," he said, slapping him firmly on the back. A small boy soon appeared from among the trees.

"I brought yer dinner, Mr. Wilkins, sir" he said. He was carrying a large basket in which was propped a large jug of cider. He put it down on a log and made as if to leave.

"Where are you off to, lad?" asked Mr. Wilkins.

"Off for me dinner, Mr. Wilkins, sir".

"No need for the 'sir', lad. Just Mr Wilkins. Now, is your ma expecting you?" The boy shook his head. "Well, sit yourself on that log. You can give us a hand this afternoon and start by helping with this food. There's more than enough." A big smile lighting up his face, the boy sat down and accepted the food that the farmer gave him. George Wilkins introduced Nathan to the boy, who looked with some awe at him, as if bursting to ask him questions about the War, and the three ate their lunch, washing it down with the still cool cider. After lunch, the work went more quickly, with Jack working hard stacking the logs for them. By the time they finished in the early evening, they had cleared quite an area.

"We'll get back to the farm," George Wilkins said, "and call it a good day's work."

Chapter Eight

And so it continued, one day following another for around four weeks as summer took more of a hold on the countryside. Sometimes George Wilkins would go out working with Nathan and young Jack Evans, and sometimes Nathan and the lad would be out on their own. The old farmer would however never fail to meet the boy each morning to ask about his grandfather's health, which thankfully seemed to improve with every passing day.

It was a busy time of the year, with the cutting of meadow grass for winter hay having to be prepared for and all the routine chores and maintenance of a farm still having to be fitted in, so it was with a big smile that George Wilkins received the news from Jack that his grandfather had finally been passed fit to return to work by Doctor Allerby. For his part, the boy seemed rather downcast by the message he'd brought. George Wilkins put his hand on the boy's shoulder.

"What's up lad? You look like you've lost sixpence and found yourself a penny."

"Well, Mr. Wilkins, I thought that as my Bampi was coming back to work, you wouldn't be wanting me any more."

"It's good news old John's coming back, my lad. He's a good worker." He paused, eyeing the boy up and down, much to the lad's discomfort. Nathan, in the background, smiled to himself. "But that's something that seems to run in your family, because I've noticed myself that you work just as hard, as well as being told by others that you do." Both Jack and the farmer glanced across at Nathan, who winked at the boy. "If you want the work, my boy, I'll be more than happy to keep you on with that grandfather of yours, at least until school starts again." A grin split the boy's face from ear to ear, and he couldn't stop thanking the farmer until he received a gruff but friendly "Now get on with your work."

Nathan and Jack had built up a rapport verging on real friendship despite the difference in their ages. As Jack had become more confident in Nathan's company, his natural inquisitiveness had come to to the fore with question after question, at first about the army in general and then about life in the trenches and the actual fighting. Nathan, unusually finding himself fairly comfortable talking to the boy about it, answered each question patiently and with as much honesty as he could, but without glamorising the subject for the boy. As for Jack, he began to regard Nathan with something close to worship.

George Wilkins' decision was good news for Jack, and Nathan was delighted for the boy, and for the Evans family, who would now have two wages coming in for a while. He'd visited John two or three times a week since the older man had been taken ill, and a close friendship had sprung up between him and the old Welshman. He knew how the old man fretted about being confined to the house by the doctor and how glad he would be to get back to work. When the day's work was over, he walked home with young Jack, and paid a short visit to John, but as the family were just about to have their supper, he didn't stay long.

Later in the evening Nathan was walking off a delicious but very filling meal prepared by Martha; casting a long shadow in the evening sun, he paused by the river for a few moments. It was turning into one of his favourite spots for a little reflection, but this evening he didn't stop long. Continuing on down the road, the raucous call of some disturbed crows accompanying him, he noticed a few fallen apples in the orchards. Autumn, not now, was the time for home baked apple pies and cider making would then be in full swing. Ahead, overgrown from a small orchard, he saw the branch of a tree reaching over into the lane, hanging heavy with still growing fruit. He couldn't resist the temptation to pick one of the apples. Just as he bit into it, pulling a face from the sharpness of the taste, a laughing voice said from behind him.

"Nice 'uns, them apples, but not ready yet." Nathan felt himself colour with guilt and had the same strong urge to run away that he'd felt so often when he was a boy. He turned to see who had spoken. A ruddy-faced man was grinning at him, leaning over a gate a little further along the lane. "Used to do that me sel', when I was a boy," he said.

"So did I, and from this orchard as well," said Nathan, now also laughing, "but I never used to get caught then," he added. Then, more mischievously, he continued. "When I lived in the village, we used to come here regularly - they were the best apples around!"

"They still are," the other man said proudly. "But that will have been before my time. I only came here a couple of years back. I'm still a newcomer as far as some of them in the village is concerned." He laughed. The two men parted, with the farmer disappearing behind the hedge once more. Nathan walked on, unwisely taking another bite from his apple, which he then threw into the hedgerow. Before he realised where he was, he saw the entrance to Smallbrook, the farm he'd seen from up on the hill with John Evans. Unconsciously, he paused by the farm gate and looked the place over.

Remembering how deserted and run-down it was when he was a boy playing here, he could see that a great deal of effort was being made to look after the place. It surprised him, because John Evans had told him that it was being run by a young woman on her own. But what surprised him more was the flower garden next to the house.

It was an amazing splash of late-spring colour, with flowers of all varieties and hues. He walked along the lane to get a better view and stood leaning on the wall, almost entranced by the brightness of the display. How on earth did a woman running a farm by herself manage to find the time to work on and tend such a lovely garden? While he considered the answer, the woman in question came out of the house and began to carefully pick dead heads from the flowers, unaware of her audience.

She'd been wearing a scarf when he'd seen her before, but even with her hair free, as she was now, Nathan recognised her with a sharp pang of guilt. She was the woman who'd been standing by the bridge the other day when he'd helped free the cart. He'd all but ignored her then, wrapped up in his own thoughts. He couldn't help but look more closely, as even with such a brief encounter he'd been struck by her pretty face. A phrase of his aunt's came to mind: 'pretty as a picture.' Slender and barely five feet tall, she moved around her garden gracefully and as he watched she seemed to be constantly pushing an unruly strand of hair back into place, and her lips were set in an unconscious pout of concentration.

His eyes followed her as she worked and suddenly it was as if she'd become aware of being watched. She looked around sharply, like some startled animal. Nathan glanced guiltily away but resisted a boyish urge to duck down behind the wall at having been caught out and turned and smiled instead. She walked slowly across to him, smoothing her long skirt without even thinking about what she was doing, and smiled back, a friendly smile that lit up her entire face, which was already warmed by the evening sun. He couldn't help but take in and appreciate her healthy demeanour and extremely attractive figure.

"Hello," said Nathan nervously as she approached him. "It's a nice evening, isn't it?" She agreed that it was. "You've a lovely garden," he continued, not really knowing what to say, but wanting to say something and feeling that he should. "How do you find the time to look after it?" She smiled again, her pale eyes twinkling with a mixture of embarrassment and suppressed laughter.

"I make the time. It means a lot me," she said. Jenny's flow of conversation then also ran dry. With both of them at a loss for words, it occurred to Nathan that he should perhaps introduce himself, which he did, awkwardly extending his hand over the wall. She shook it gently, forgetting to remove her gardening gloves.

"Thank you, Mr. Holt. My name is Jenny Tiley and I'm very pleased to meet you. I saw you helping at the bridge the other day. You're new to the village aren't you?"

"Not really. I used to live here in the village when I was a boy. I'm staying at The Lamb now. And I owe you an apology for the other day. It was rude of me not to speak" Jenny nodded and the conversation dried up again. Nathan excused himself by saying that he must get on his way. Jenny smiled and wishing him a good evening, turned back to her flowers. Nathan made his way back to the village with a lot on his mind.

Chapter Nine

The cutting of the grass in the meadows was a busy time on a farm. In readiness for the inevitable coming of winter, farmers had to ensure sufficient hay and feed for their livestock, enough to last even the longest and harshest winter. The vale itself was not prone to hard winters but there had been times, within the memory of some of the older inhabitants, when because of heavy falls of snow the village had been cut off for two or three days at a time, with wagons and carts unable to descend into the villages or to climb from them. As if the thought of the approaching winter were not enough for the farmers, there was the problem of who would do the work. For the last two or three years there had been only the very young, the very old or the infirm to help with farm work - the war had seen to that. It meant that at busy times everyone in the village who could help did, as it was the only way that everything would be done in time.

It was no different for Jenny Tiley and Smallbrook. Although in the beginning both she and Edward had worried as to how she would manage, everything had worked out fine. Heavy horses and mowing equipment had been hired from their landlord, George Wilkins, who had provided a man to help as well, a hard worker although almost into his seventies, Harry Mason. He was a small dynamo of a man who worked the land all of his life and could not and would not give it up. Jenny had taken to him immediately as nothing seemed capable of removing the smile from his wrinkled face. Edward had been more reserved with the old countryman, treating him more like paid help than Jenny liked.

A popular man around Dalton Combe, Harry had a sick wife, and was able to work part-time for George Wilkins only through the help of his neighbours in giving their time to assist in looking after her. When news of Edward's death had filtered through the village, Harry had discussed the situation with his wife, and the couple had decided to offer what help they could to Jenny, not wanting to see her forced to leave Smallbrook when she so plainly wanted to make a go of the place. A brief argument had ensued between Jenny and Harry over money, with Harry not wanting anything from her, and with Jenny, on the other hand, not wanting this kindly old man to help her for no payment. As far as she was concerned, if she was to have his help, she would have to find the money to pay for it. It was her only way of hanging on to Smallbrook. In the end, Harry had given in, and Jenny got her way.

She had on more than one occasion been grateful she'd accepted his offer; Harry Mason was a great help around the place, coming to her whenever his part time work on the Wilkins Manor Farm allowed. Despite his age, he easily handled all of the heavy work and organised the harvest for her, as she simply was not strong enough to handle the two heavy shire horses she always hired from Mr Wilkins. He was nothing short of a gift from Heaven.

It was still early in the morning, but Jenny had milked her small herd of cows and let them back out into the meadow and was sitting quietly drinking a cup of tea. Harry normally joined her unless it was a cheese making morning, because then there were no milk churns to be shifted for collection, and she didn't need his help until later in the day. Drinking the tea slowly and savouring every drop, she suddenly thought to herself that Harry was a little late, but then she heard his familiar light tap on the door.

"Come on in, Harry. The tea's still hot" she called out. As soon as she saw him, Jenny knew there was something wrong. Usually a bright cheery person, he looked worried and dejected.

"Mornin, Mrs. Tiley," he said. Jenny smiled. No amount of coaxing on her part would ever make Harry call her Jenny. He sat down at the table, placing his cap next to the mug of tea that she was already pouring for him.

"'Morning, Harry," she replied jauntily, knowing that it just wouldn't do for her to directly ask if there was anything wrong. They sat in silence for some minutes, while Harry avoided looking her in the eyes. Finally, Jenny could stand it no longer. "How's your wife, Harry?" she asked politely, trying to start a conversation with him. The sudden look of sorrow on his face told her all she needed to know. "Harry? Is there a problem?"

"She's been taken real bad this time, Missus Tiley," he said, still staring uncomfortably into his tea. "Doctor reckons she shouldn't be left on 'er own too much now. It means I won't be able to come 'ere for you no more." The last sentence was almost blurted out. Jenny felt close to tears, but not for herself. Harry looked so sad. "I've already been up to Mr. Wilkins at the Manor to tell 'im the same thing."

"Oh, Harry. Is there anything I can do? How will you

manage?"

"It'll be 'ard, but we'll get by. We allus 'ave done, and we allus will. " He smiled. "We've our old age pension to live on each week." Jenny almost cried. Since the old age pension had been introduced by Lloyd George some years earlier, it meant that couples like Harry and his wife no longer had to worry about the awful spectre of the workhouse when they could no longer work, But it was still not a lot to live on. Jenny reached over the table and took his hand in hers.

"Harry, if there's anything I can do..." Her voice trailed off. He shook his head.

"That's very good of you, Missus Tiley, I allus knew you was a good 'un." He looked slightly embarrassed, and drained his tea cup. He stood up and Jenny walked across to the kitchen door with him. As he opened the door, she took his hand in hers.

"Wait a second, Harry." She crossed to the kitchen and took two half-crowns from her jug. Walking back to the door, she pressed them into Harry's hand. "Thanks for all your help, Harry. I don't know what I'd have done if you hadn't come along." She kissed him lightly on the cheek. "Now, before you even start to think it," she said more briskly, "let's have no worrying about me. You save all that for when you need it. I'll be fine. Your wife is the most important thing for you. Look after her and get her well."

"Missus Tiley, I can't take these," he said glancing at his hand, his eyes moist.

"Yes you can, and you will, Harry." She watched him walk slowly across the farmyard and only when he'd disappeared along the lane did she turn and go back into the farm kitchen, where she slumped into a chair and let her head sink to the scrubbed table.

Time for cutting the meadow grass was upon her, the weather was perfect and she knew she couldn't manage the work by herself. To give her small herd enough food for the winter, the grass would have to be cut in the lower meadow within the next few days. It was too large to cut by hand and she couldn't manage a team of horses. Possibly if she asked in the village if anyone needed work someone might help, but then realised sadly that the men in the area were fully occupied and there was no one available. She was confident that Mr Wilkins would be able to advise her, but there was too much to do to spare the time for a visit at the moment.

She was still sitting thinking about her problems when she heard noises outside in the farmyard. Rising to her feet and opening the kitchen door she was surprised to see Nathan Holt, the pleasant young man she'd been talking to a few evenings before, leading two shire horses and mowing equipment across the yard towards the gate to the meadow. He was walking with a noticeable limp, almost dragging his left leg. That must be as a result of the wound Harry had told her about. Sitting on the mower with an air of importance was a young boy whose name she couldn't remember, but who she recognised from the village. The boy waved as she appeared, and the young man nodded in her direction.

"Nathan Holt and his young assistant Jack Evans, at your service, ma'am," he said with a smile and a mock bow, stopping the horses. As she looked a little confused, he quickly continued and explained. "Old Harry Mason came to Manor Farm early this morning to see Mr. Wilkins. He seemed quite upset, not his normal self at all. Well, after he'd gone, Mr. Wilkins came across to young Jack here and me and said our plans for the day were changed. We were to harness up the horses to the mower and get down here to get your meadow cut. It seems Harry can't do it this year, although Mr. Wilkins didn't tell us why." Jenny looked up at him as he spoke and he was happy to see a smile light up her own face, which had been a little drawn and worried when she'd first come to the door.

"Did he say anything else?" She was a little worried she might have to pay for this work.

"Oh yes," said Nathan, his eyes twinkling. "He said he'd rather have two lazy buggers like us working for you than sitting around on our backsides all day." Jack, up on the mower, giggled.

"It were a bit worse than that, Missus Tiley," the boy said. She couldn't help but laugh with them both.

"So here we are," said Nathan, as the laughter subsided, "and where do we start?" Jenny pointed to the gate at the bottom end of the farmyard, in the direction they had already been going.

"Over there across the stream," she said. "It's usually cut starting in the top corner near the woods, and then worked back towards the farm."

"That'll do for me," said Nathan. "At least the stream's not running through the middle of the meadow," he added. "Well, we'd better be getting on, Mrs Tiley, if that's alright with you." She said it was, and watched as they carefully negotiated the farmyard and the gate out into the meadow, and then went back to her kitchen.

The mowing went well in the meadow, a steady tramp back and forth across the field for man, boy and horses, and was uneventful apart from one or two unexpected humps and bumps, none of any consequence to the horses, but one of which did threaten to unseat Jack from his perch. It was his job to guide the horses, while Nathan kept a steady eye on the mowing machinery, watching out for problems and possible jams. With only part of his mind occupied in his task, the rest of it was free to roam, but for the first part of the morning it didn't seem to get any further than the old counting song he remembered learning at school: 'One man went to mow, went to mow a meadow...' over and over again.

Half-way through the morning, with almost a third of the field cut, Nathan unharnessed the horses and had Jack lead them to the stream for a drink. As the boy returned with them, Nathan was surprised to see Jenny appear from the farmhouse with what turned out to be a jug of lemonade and a plate of warm buttered bread.

"It's fresh baked this morning," she explained as she brought it to them, "and I thought you might both need something cool to drink." Jack leapt on the beautiful smelling bread as if he hadn't eaten for a week, while Nathan was only a little more reticent. They both thanked a smiling Jenny with their mouths

71

stuffed with bread, but Nathan felt a little disappointed when she returned to the farmhouse, leaving them to their mid-morning snack.

With only a short stop later for their lunch, this time eating food they'd brought themselves, Nathan and Jack had finished the field by the middle of the afternoon, leaving row after row of aromatic cut grass behind them. While Jack watered the horses once more, Nathan looked thoughtfully at the field. He was still thoughtful when he tapped lightly on the farmhouse door to tell Jenny they had finished.

"How are you going to collect up all that grass?" he asked her. "It's a lot of work." It was a question Jenny had been asking herself.

"Harry did it for me last year," she replied.

"By himself?"

"Yes. It took him a few days, but he got all the grass into the barn for me." She paused and unconsciously pushed a straying strand of hair back into place. It was a gesture he was already becoming familiar with. "But he won't be able to do it this year," she continued. Nathan looked surprised. He knew that Harry had been upset this morning but had no idea why.

"Why not?"

"His wife's ill and has taken a turn for the worse, and he needs to be with her. He won't be able to help me out any more, and that's what he told Mr. Wilkins earlier."

"Do you have any other help?" he asked. She shook her

head, loosening the strand of hair again.

"No, it's all down to me until I can find somebody," she answered.

Chapter Ten

Nathan was still thoughtful as he and Jack walked the horses and mowing equipment back into the main yard at Manor Farm. Delegating the boy to see to the horses, he took for himself the task of clearing grass out of the mower and cleaning and oiling its moving parts. His thoughts were still revolving around the problems at Smallbrook, and, he had to admit to himself, although he wouldn't have done to anyone else, more than just a little bit with Jenny Tiley.

The girls he'd met or come into contact with while in the army, usually in pubs, dance-halls or variety theatres, were quite brash, outgoing and definitely fun-loving. Jenny Tiley was different in so many ways. He could see she was self-confident and capable, but he thought he could also detect a very attractive shyness and vulnerability about her. And there was no denying she was a very pretty young woman. A sharp pain in his thumb caused him to jerk his hand away from the blade he'd just started sharpening, and he sucked at the blood that was beginning to appear.

"Damn!" he muttered, cursing himself for not concentrating on what he was doing.

"How did it go today, Nathan?" George Wilkins was standing at the doorway of the huge stone barn where the machinery was stored, the late afternoon sun casting his shadow across the floor and leaving him almost in silhouette.

"It's all cut and drying in the field, Mr. Wilkins, though God alone knows how she'll manage to get it all collected up and into her barn," he replied.

"You know about Harry, then?"

"Yes. Mrs. Tiley told me," said Nathan, in between sucking his thumb, which did not seem to want to stop bleeding.

"Harry was a godsend to that girl," Wilkins said, "and a damned good worker for me. It's going to be difficult for her." There was quite a long silence, during which it occurred to Nathan that George Wilkins might just be hinting at the very subject he was thinking of broaching himself. The old farmer's next comment seemed to confirm that suspicion. "She's certainly going to need some help at Smallbrook, but I don't know where she's going to get it from." This was followed by another long silence, with neither of them looking at the other, and both seeming to expect the other to say something. Nathan slowly straightened up from where he'd been bending over the mower and looked at George Wilkins.

"Is there no one who can help?" he asked. George Wilkins shook his head.

"No one I can think of. It'll mean she won't be able to keep the farm on of course, and for me it'll be a shame to lose such a good tenant, and hard to find someone to take on a small farm like Smallbrook in these difficult times."

"Tenant?" Nathan was genuinely surprised.

"Yes, and the place will soon fall into wrack and ruin again without someone there." Nathan nodded. He had clear memories of what the place used to look like. "It would be a kindness if someone would help her and a personal favour to me as well."

"To you?"

"Well, think about it, lad." Nathan had still not quite got used to George Wilkins referring to him as 'lad.' "It's to my benefit if the farm is tenanted, working and well looked after," George Wilkins said. It gave Nathan something to think about. There was another silence, with Nathan deep in thought. He certainly didn't notice the old farmer smiling.

"Would it be any good if I was to help her out?" Nathan asked. George Wilkins burst out laughing and slapped Nathan on the back.

"Well it took you long enough to offer," he explained. "I've been giving it some thought all day, but I didn't want to ask you or tell you to do it. I wanted you to offer, and hard work you made of it." He became more serious." You'll be doing both me and Mrs Tiley a great favour Nathan. I'd like to see the girl succeed and you're a good worker." He held out his hand and shook Nathan's vigorously. "Thank you, but she's not to know what I think. That's between us. I can't have her thinking her landlord's gone all soft. It's just between us. Agreed?" Nathan nodded, not really understanding why the old farmer would want to be so reticent about his help. With another firm shake of the hand, Wilkins released Nathan's hand and with a big smile and another "Thank you" left the barn. A little stunned at the turn of events, Nathan finished sharpening the blades of the mower without inflicting any further cuts on himself, and resolved to make a detour to Smallbrook Farm on his way back to The Lamb when he'd finished for the day.

Later, standing in the small porch by the farmhouse door, Nathan found himself actually feeling a little nervous, almost as if he was a suitor calling on his girl for the first time. He took a deep breath and from his vantage point cast his eye around the place before knocking. He had taken little notice in the morning, his mind occupied with the mowing and slightly distracted by Jenny herself. The farmyard itself was untidy and cluttered with rusting implements left leaning against the walls. It showed every sign of becoming run down, but not, Nathan suspected, through neglect or any lack of effort on the owner's part. He'd already formed the impression that Smallbrook meant more to Jenny Tiley than anything else. There were certainly jobs around the farm which could keep him busy and he found himself absently starting to plan what should be done first. Coming back to himself, he tapped on the solid looking kitchen door. There was no response. He knocked again, but still nothing.

Not knowing what to do, he tried the door and found it open. This was no real surprise as hardly anybody locked their doors during the daytime. He called out loudly from the kitchen, but no-one replied. Then it occurred to him that Mrs Tiley might be out around the farm somewhere and where better for him to start looking than the milking shed. It was still early and she might not have finished with the cows. And that is where he found her moments later, sitting on a milking stool. She was wearing a scarf around her hair and had her head pressed into a cow's flank as she coaxed the last drops of milk from the creature's almost empty udder. He could hear her softly singing to her self as she worked, unaware of his presence, and he waited a few moments before coughing loudly. She looked around, startled.

"Good evening Mrs. Tiley. I'm sorry, I didn't mean to make you jump," he said. "I seem to be making a bit of a habit of it."

"No, that's alright. It's just that I wasn't expecting anybody." His sudden appearance in the doorway of the milking shed had shaken her a little. "Let me just finish with Charlotte here." There was no more milk to be had from this particular cow, and all the others had been milked, so she eased herself up from the stool and carefully eased the bucket from underneath the animal. Nathan reached out and took it from her as she straightened up, a little wearily, he thought. His eyebrows were raised a little as she caught his eye to thank him.

"Charlotte?" he asked, smiling. She reddened a little.

"Oh yes, they've all got names. They're more like friends." She paused, reddening further, realising how silly she might be sounding to him. Farmers weren't supposed to become too attached to their animals. She tried to explain. "I only keep them for the milk."

"What happens when they grow too old for milk?" Nathan asked, smiling a little more.

"It hasn't happened yet," she said, a big smile lighting up her face. It faded as she added "but I suppose it will. I don't think I could let the butchers have them for meat, though. I wouldn't be able to eat it". The honking of a goose interrupted them temporarily and they both looked to the doorway.

"And I suppose all your animals have names?" His smile was becoming slightly mischievous. She noticed the tone in his

79

voice.

"You're making fun of me, but yes they have." She was about to continue when he held his hand up to stop her.

"No need to tell me. I'm sure I'll get to know them if you take me on to help."

"Take you on to help?" Jenny repeated his words, her mind in a whirl, not really understanding, but hoping that she really was hearing what she thought she was. "I don't need... I can't pay..." Nathan interrupted again, seeing her obvious embarrassment and confusion.

"Money's no issue, Mrs. Tiley. I'm still being paid by the army – for now, anyway. I'd heard that you needed some help here..." He paused as he saw her face cloud slightly with pride fighting necessity. Nathan hoped that necessity would be the winner. He was as aware as she was that she could not manage Smallbrook on her own. Giving herself time to think, she said

"If you can wait until I've cleaned up here, can we talk about it over a cup of tea?" He nodded.

"Do you want me to let the cows loose while I'm waiting?" he asked. A smile gave him all the answer he needed.

The offer of a cup of tea to talk about Nathan's offer was for Jenny a smokescreen. She knew she needed help and was ready to accept this offer from Nathan, who seemed to her after their few very brief meetings to be a very pleasant and friendly person. The idea of the chat was to spend just a little more time with him and find out if she was right. She watched him working at helping her clean out the milking shed, noticing once more the ease in all his movements apart from his leg and his patient way with the cows. She found herself feeling comfortable with him. Nathan, after initial nervousness, was feeling the same, and was already thinking before the cup of tea that she would accept his offer. Both were ready for the drink after they'd finished.

In the kitchen, Nathan found his nerves returning. Working alongside this pretty young woman was one thing; making conversation was another. He began to feel uncomfortable as she boiled the kettle and then was embarrassed as she caught him watching when she shook her hair free from her headscarf and ran her fingers through it to untangle it slightly. A little embarrassed herself about the attention, she hurriedly began to talk about not only the work that needed doing around the farm but also some of her plans and ideas. She found Nathan a receptive listener and was pleased to hear him offering some suggestions. Before either of them knew it, evening was turning into dusk and Nathan mentioned he should leave. His parting comment seemed to assume that her acceptance of his offer was taken as given.

"Goodnight, and I'll see you in the morning."

Chapter Eleven

The next morning saw Nathan tapping on Jenny's door at Smallbrook, feeling an uneasy nervousness he didn't understand. She answered his knock quickly as if she had been expecting it, and offered him a cup of tea, which he accepted gratefully after his walk from the village. While she was pouring it, he said that unless anything urgent needed doing, he'd make a start on getting the grass into the barn while the weather held. He was slightly taken aback when she laughingly told him that half the day was gone already – the cows had been milked, the poultry fed and the pigs and the geese already foraging in the orchard.

"Was it nice to stay in bed on your first day?" she asked, a huge mischievous smile on her face, a smile that Nathan missed, gazing uncomfortably at the table and not looking at Jenny. By the time he looked up, the smile and the twinkle in her eyes had gone as she realised she might have inadvertently upset him.

"We didn't talk about what time I'd be starting," he said, slightly embarrassed. "I just came along after breakfast at The Lamb. If you'd wanted me earlier..." He didn't have a chance to finish speaking before Jenny interrupted him, her joking having backfired.

"I didn't mean you should have been earlier. I'm sorry. I was trying to make a joke. Shall we start again?" He nodded, relieved. While he continued drinking his tea, but still not wanting to look her in the face, she told him about a large handcart in the barn, which needed some repairs. "It's what Harry used last year for bringing in the grass," she explained.

Nathan found the cart in surprisingly good repair, despite what Jenny had told him. He'd been concerned it might be irreparable or unusable. A little drop of oil on the axle, a few nails and some fresh pieces of wood and it was ready. Not as good as new, but ready for use. Wheeling it up to the field, taking a rake and a pitch-fork with him, Nathan began to relax a little and started work on the grass that had been cut the previous day. Working from the same corner in which he and young Jack had started cutting, he was happy to find that the grass had already had a chance to start drying out in the hot weather. It turned out to be harder work than he'd expected and he'd only taken his third cartload into the barn when Jenny appeared in the barn doorway.

"It's lunch time Nathan. Do you want something to eat?" He hadn't thought about food, but realised he was ravenously hungry. "I've got something ready in the kitchen, just bread cheese and pickle. Come in when you're ready." She smiled and turned away, and he thought to himself that he must be hot and sweaty after a morning's work. Stripping off his shirt, he walked across the farmyard to the water pump and dowsed himself in the cool water. He immediately felt fresher, if a little wet, with nothing at hand to dry himself with, so he used his shirt, drying his chest and arms before towelling his hair dry, before slipping it back on and turning towards the kitchen door. He smiled broadly at Jenny who seemed a little embarrassed at having been caught watching him. She still seemed slightly flushed as he walked through the door.

They began their meal in a slightly uncomfortable silence, despite their long companionable chat the previous evening. Jenny found herself nervous about eating with a man her own age, as it had never been a problem with Harry. Nathan, for his part, was used to finding himself tongue tied around young women. Questions about the farm from him and about how he was getting on up in the field from her eased things while they were drinking their tea, and when they'd finished, Nathan was surprised to see Jenny simply pile their plates and mugs in the sink and tie her hair up in a scarf. She caught the look on his face.

"I'm coming out to help," she explained. They spoke little while they worked, but Nathan took great pleasure from her amiable companionship and friendly smiles. With her raking up the grass into piles and Nathan forking the piles into the cart, it considerably cut down the time it took to do the work. He had Jenny's help until it was time to milk the cows from which time Nathan worked alone until the approach of dusk. Jenny was waiting for him in the kitchen doorway after he had put the cart and tools away. They parted reluctantly with a few words, and Nathan found himself not wanting to walk away down the lane. Jenny watched him from the doorway until he disappeared from view, wishing that he'd stayed a little longer, if only for a cup of tea.

Unusually for her, Jenny had a fitful and uneasy night's sleep, disturbed in particular by a strange dream about her husband Edward, the first she'd had since hearing of his death.

He came walking towards her across the farmyard, his arms outstretched as if to cuddle her. This was out of character in itself for a man unaccustomed to showing his feelings and emotions, but seemed perfectly natural to her in the dream as she ran to him. He folded his arms protectively around her and she rested her head on his shoulder, feeling his warm breath on her neck. Then she looked up – into Nathan's smiling face, not Edward's. It felt so right to be secure and warm in his arms. Then she'd woken to sunlight flooding through her bedroom window, still somehow feeling safe and reassured, if just a little guilty because it had been Nathan and not Edward. She was still unsettled when Nathan arrived, greeting him a little sheepishly as if there was some way he could've known about the dream and feeling almost relieved when he said he intended to set to work on gathering in the remainder of the grass immediately after washing out the milking shed, a job he had insisted on taking over from Jenny. Even so, as he turned away to the barn, she watched him and briefly wondered how it would feel to have his arms around her. Then she dismissed the thought as silly and foolish – she had chores to do. After all, it was butter-making day.

Nathan and Jenny worked separately throughout the morning, but shared their lunch in the farmhouse kitchen. Instead of joining Nathan in the field as she'd done the previous day, Jenny loaded up her bicycle with butter and set off for Dalton Combe. Nathan paused in his work and watched her cycle away. He had the strange feeling that in Jenny's absence, the afternoon was going to drag by. As if to confirm his worry, he couldn't settle to his work properly, happy thoughts of Jenny helping him the day before in and out of his mind like a butterfly he couldn't quite catch hold of. Normally he was happy alone, enjoying being solitary, but today felt unsettled, missing her company.

He was just coming out of the barn, having emptied another cart-load of grass when he heard the tinkling sound of a bicycle bell, and smiled to himself as Jenny was obviously announcing her return to the farm. He was surprised to feel a little flutter of excitement at seeing her. She'd dismounted from the bicycle in the lane, for some reason not wanting to dismount in front of Nathan but when she saw his warm welcoming smile, she had to resist a mad desire to drop the machine to the floor and throw her arms around him. Flushing slightly at the thought, she turned and leaned the bicycle against the farmhouse wall.

"How was Mr. Williams?" he asked, feeling that he would much rather be saying something more interesting, but not knowing what.

"He tried to over-pay me, as usual," she said, smiling. She could sense Nathan's discomfort, but was equally uncomfortable.

"Over-pay you?" Nathan was genuinely surprised.

"Oh, he always tries to give me more money than he should. I think it's his way of trying to help me now I'm on my own," she replied. "How have you been getting on without me?" she continued innocently, putting the slight flush on his face down to him being hot.

"I should have finished collecting up the grass tomorrow,"

he said. "Joshua says we're in for rain soon, so it'll be just in time. Then it's just a matter of getting it all into the hayloft." Jenny simply nodded, and Nathan, suddenly keen to be back in the field, turned away with the hand-cart. This beautiful weather couldn't last and no matter how much they wished it not to be so, autumn and winter would inevitably come. Jenny, still slightly shaken from her desire to hug Nathan tightly, walked into the shade of the kitchen and sat down. It felt comfortable and normal to have a man around the farm, but it was arousing emotions she thought had died. Most of all, she just wanted a man to hold her.

Chapter Twelve

The hayloft was uncomfortably warm and forking the hay around was proving hot work. Nathan had considered that gathering the grass in to the barn had been hard work, but getting it up into the hayloft was proving almost unbearable. He was stripped to the waist, but still the sweat was running down his torso. This was not September weather, he thought irritably. The rain prophesied by Joshua hadn't appeared and if anything, the weather had become warmer. There was no air moving in the barn at all.

"Nathan!" Jenny's voice interrupted his thoughts.

"Up here!" he called back. "If you wait a minute, I'll be down."

"No, you wait there. I'll come up." Moments later, she appeared at the top of the steps, clutching a jug and two mugs. "I brought you a drink." As she poured them both some cider, Nathan carefully propped the pitchfork against the wall. "You look hot," she said, suddenly not knowing whether or not to look at his muscular half-naked body. Nathan, for his part, self-consciously reached for his shirt.

"No, you don't have to, if you're too hot." She felt the colour rise in her cheeks as she said it. This is ridiculous, she thought to herself. I was a married woman, why should it bother me? But bother her it certainly did. Nathan, taking a deep drink from his mug and savouring the cool taste of the cider, noticed an air of innocence and shyness about Jenny he was sure he hadn't seen before. She seemed vulnerable, so different to the self confident

89

woman who ran a farm by herself.

Although he'd obviously noticed Jenny was far from being a plain-looking woman, he'd not really taken in just how attractive she was. Now, as she sat with him in the hayloft with her hair slightly dishevelled, and a face flushed from the heat, Nathan found he could hardly take his eyes from her. He sat and gazed into his mug, suddenly as uncomfortable as she was.

"You've been working hard, Nathan. You've done so much since you started coming to Smallbrook." To Jenny, this sounded like she was forcing the conversation, saying something just to try to ease the tension which she was sure they'd both noticed had appeared between them from nowhere.

"You wouldn't have been able to do it by yourself," Nathan said. It sounded like a criticism, but he'd not meant it to. They lapsed into silence, broken only when he'd drained his mug. "Is there any more cider in that jug?"

She nodded, stood up and leaned over to pour more of the cold cider into his mug. As she turned her face towards him, Nathan impulsively kissed her mouth, tasting the cider on her lips. She pulled away sharply, spilling a little cider from the jug, not looking at him.

"I'm sorry...," he began. "I shouldn't have done that."

"No, no, it's alright," Jenny said, colouring and surprised by what had happened, but silently cursing herself for pulling away. It had been a very pleasant kiss. The tension in the hayloft was now almost unbearable. "I'd better get back to the kitchen, there's lots to be done." She started towards the steps. Nathan stood and put his hands on her shoulders, stopping her and turning her around to face him.

"Jenny...," he began. She turned into his arms, looking up at him and smiling. He kissed her again and this time she responded more eagerly. His arms felt as strong as she'd imagined and she seemed to just melt into his body. Neither of them were aware of the simple act of taking their clothes off and Nathan, feeling his love and excitement for her rising until he could help himself no longer, pulled her gently down onto the pile of soft warm grass. Their bodies joined and they were soon moving in an easy rhythm as they explored their bodies, each enjoying the feel of the other. Afternoon drifted into early evening as they slept in each other's arms and it was Jenny who woke first, sitting up sharply.

"The cows!" she exclaimed, rapidly pulling on her clothes. She was halfway down the steep wooden stairs almost before Nathan realised she'd gone. He dressed and followed her. Life on a farm doesn't even give way to romance, he reflected wryly as walked across the farmyard following her.

The milking finished, they returned to the farmhouse, where Jenny put a kettle on to boil for some tea. Neither knew what to say about what had happened in the hayloft, but the silence between them was a comfortable one. Both knew their relationship had moved on irrevocably. Over the tea, Jenny said she'd like to cook for Nathan, and he readily agreed, but only if he could finish her chores around the farm while she was preparing the meal. Persuading the geese, chickens and ducks that it was time to return to their pens was easier than he thought it would be – food proved a good incentive. The pigs were more of a problem. It seemed that they'd decided spending the night in the orchard was preferable to being shut up in their pen. By the time he'd cornered them, Jenny was calling for him to come and eat.

The meal was simple and tasty, and while they were eating Nathan made her laugh more than once telling her about how difficult it had been to catch the pigs. Then she suddenly became serious and reached across the table, putting her hand over his.

"Nathan, please stay," she said quietly.

"Stay?" he asked.

"Yes. Here. Tonight." She hoped she didn't sound too shameless to him, but was relieved to be rewarded with a smile. He didn't know what to say.

"I'll stay," he answered, his heart beating a little faster as he said the words. She squeezed his hand and then collected the dishes and put them in the sink, her thoughts in turmoil about what she'd just done.

She'd had a bath. Gallantly, Nathan had stayed out of the kitchen while she washed herself, and now, dressed in her nightdress, she appeared in the doorway of the parlour. Nathan looked at her, vulnerable and very very desirable and smiled. She settled herself next to him, cuddling up and his heart leapt at the closeness of her. She felt clean and warm to him, her hair especially, and he buried his face in it, nuzzling her neck, breathing in deeply, simply enjoying her freshness. He slipped his arm around her. She was shivering slightly.

"Are you cold?" he asked gently. She shook her head and responded, pulling away slightly and turning her head until her lips found his. Nathan ran his fingers down her body, following her curves.

"No, just hold me," she said almost sleepily. "Hold me tight." Her breathing, warm on his shoulder, slowed and deepened and she was soon sound asleep, cradled in his arms.

The soft light of dawn woke Nathan hours later, aching and cold in the early morning chill, still holding Jenny in his arms. He rubbed his eyes blearily with one hand, not wishing to let go of her warm body with the other in case he woke her. The light from the two small sash windows was enough for him to make out her outline and he looked down at her face, content and half-smiling, and with one finger brushed her usual strand of wayward hair back into place. Then he lightly ran his fingers over the silky smoothness of her bare shoulder, and down to trace the gentle rise and fall of her breasts in rhythm with her breathing through the fabric of her nightdress.

"Mmm, that feels nice," she murmured sleepily, not opening her eyes. He carried on gently for a few minutes, and then whispered softly in her ear

"I'll make some tea."

"No," she whispered back, eyes still closed, "not yet," and raising her head kissed him gently and then more passionately. He responded and with a little wriggling, they were soon holding each other in a much more loving embrace. As the passion increased, it took only moments for Jenny to slip out of her nightdress and just a little longer for Nathan to take off the clothes he'd slept in. Exploring their bodies, they came to know each other on a gentle wave of love that exploded into a needy rapture. The increasingly bright golden morning sunlight seemed a perfect companion to their love-making and an extra glow to their spent passion. It seemed to Jenny to be a perfect way to start the day.

Chapter Thirteen

Telling Martha that he was going to live and work at Smallbrook
Farm and be with Jenny was harder than Nathan had
anticipated. He broached the subject in the pub kitchen a few
days after starting to stay at the farm. Joshua took the news
calmly and in a very matter-of-fact fashion. He'd wished him well
and then gone out as he usually did to clean the bar and brew
some more ale. He was surprised to find that Martha was
delighted for him.

"Of course we'll miss you," she said. "It's been a real tonic
having someone different to talk to." In his weeks at The Lamb,
Nathan had been made to feel at home, like part of the family
and he would miss the friendly – and sometimes not-so-friendly –
exchanges between Martha and Joshua. "She seems a lovely
young woman, that Mrs Tiley, not that I've had much to do with
her." Nathan smiled. Martha sounded just like a mother and for
that reason, he gave her a hug and a kiss and smiled again
when he saw a flush appear on her cheeks.

"I'll still be in to see you when I fancy a pint," he said
laughing. Martha laughed with him, and then turned serious.

"You have thought about this, haven't you, Nathan. I know
it's none of my business, but I'm sure it's the question your aunt
Lily would have been asking. People will talk. You'll not be
married and tongues will wag at you living under the same roof."
Her words came tumbling out as if she was saying something

she didn't want to but knew she had to. Nathan couldn't help but hear the concern in her voice.

"We've talked about it, Martha, and it doesn't matter. Jenny needs help on that farm, or she'll lose it."

"It might not matter now, but it will, Nathan, if not for you, then for Jenny. Village gossip can be an awful thing to live with." She could see that his mind was made up and he was going to see it through, but still felt she should voice her concerns.

"I know, Martha and so does Jenny. There are people everywhere who like nothing better than to gossip about somebody else. I can handle it if it happens." The question of whether or not Jenny could handle it was left unanswered. "The important thing is that Jenny doesn't have to leave Smallbrook and that I stand by her," he added.

"Jenny Tiley doesn't know how lucky a woman she is having you," said Martha, giving him another motherly hug. He returned the hug with a tight squeeze.

"Thanks for everything, Martha, it's been like coming home." He reached down for his kit bag. Straightening up he saw tears beginning to form in Martha's eyes. With a wink and a confident smile, and pretending not to notice, he walked through to the bar, where Joshua was still wiping down tables.

"You're off then, are you lad?" he said, looking around, but continuing to clean. Nathan nodded, and Joshua straightened up from the table he had been vigorously polishing and held out his hand. "Martha may not have said it, Nathan, but there's always a place for you here if you need it." His grip was tight.

"I just told Martha I'll be back for the odd pint," Nathan said, hoping the smile on his face was hiding the fact that he was going to miss Joshua and his wife. Despite his army career, Nathan had never become used to partings.

"As I said, good luck to you lad, and there'll be a pint on me for you when you do," the landlord said. He slapped the younger man on the back and watched him walk out into the market place. Once outside, Nathan swung his kit bag up onto his shoulder and with a lighter step than he'd had in a long, long time, walked down the lane to Smallbrook and Jenny.

Chapter Fourteen

As Martha had predicted, gossip quickly spread in Dalton Combe about the relationship between Jenny and Nathan, just as it does anywhere when unusual situations arise or when behaviour moves away from what's normally accepted. It seems that no one ever knows where whispers start, but from nothing they grow to be the sole topic of conversation whenever people gather together.

The village shop, almost as much as the church or the pub, was a convenient place for social meetings. It was usually a busy, noisy place, full of chattering female voices, with the voice of shopkeeper Thomas Williams normally prominent among them. A small, wiry man, with receding dark brown hair, he wore a permanent friendly smile despite having been a widower for some years. Chatting to his customers was probably the part of his job he enjoyed the most. Unfortunately over the past few days, he felt that the idle village chatter he enjoyed so much had turned rather ugly.

With the situation at Smallbrook Farm becoming common knowledge, the subject was inevitably the perceived disreputable behaviour of Jenny Tiley. Thomas liked Jenny Tiley very much, and felt for her and the problems she'd found herself faced with when she'd heard about her husband's death. The way she'd overcome them in the time since was to his way of thinking, much to be admired. She was hardly what could be described by any normal-thinking person as a 'loose woman.' He'd met the young man, Nathan Holt, only a few times, but in Thomas' opinion he seemed a straightforward and honest person. That he was now living at Smallbrook and helping Jenny out with the work was, in his mind, a very good thing. If anything should happen to develop between the two of them, then that too was a good thing. They were both young, healthy and free of responsibilities. But the situation of them living together unmarried was, he realised, something out of the ordinary and uncomfortable for the village and many of the villagers. Being very much a man who had avoided confrontation for most of his life, and who also felt quite rightly that being argumentative with his customers could only be bad for his business, Thomas Williams kept his thoughts to himself. People, particularly those prone to idle gossip, could be high minded and the fact that his was the only shop in the village other than the butcher and the baker, would matter very little. He generally considered that such people are 'as likely to cut their noses off to spite their face as not.' As a consequence, he kept quiet and took no part in the conversations when the gossip started about Jenny Tiley. But it had become worse, today in the shop being the latest example of comments being churned over and over.

"It's not right, you know, that young woman's behaving like a hussy." This was Miss Pusey starting it off. She was an elderly spinster who lived with her equally elderly sister on the edge of the village, and had probably, thought Mr. Williams rather uncharitably, never known the affections of anyone of the male sex. "And she's never to be seen in church, nor that young soldier of hers." There were nods of agreement from some of the other female customers. Thomas sighed. How short their memories were he thought, concentrating harder on tidying up his shelves. Jenny Tiley and her late husband had been regular church-goers. It was grief stopping her going to church.

"And her husband dead less than a year, as well," said another, the voice that of Sally Adams, a sharp tongued woman at the best of times. The shopkeeper, still with his back to the shop, knew the women would all be nodding their heads at each comment just like chickens in a farmyard pecking corn. The conversation continued animatedly with none of the customers, all of whom had been served, seeming anxious to leave. The bell above the shop door tinkled merrily announcing the arrival of yet another customer and Mr. Williams turned around, a smile already in place on his face for whoever the newcomer might be. The women rapidly fell silent as Jenny Tiley, the subject of their gossiping, walked through the door.

"Good afternoon, Mrs. Tiley," he said pleasantly. "What can I do for you today?"

"Just some tea and some sugar, please Mr. Williams." Her usual open smile, which normally brightened up his shop so much, was a little faded at the sight of all the women, and he felt she looked uncomfortable at the almost palpable silence from the other customers, none of whom addressed her or even acknowledged her presence.

"I'll get those for you right away, Mrs. Tiley. "Will there be anything else?" he asked. She looked thoughtful and slightly worried as if there was something that she was uneasy asking for in the presence of the other customers.

"Yes, a double twist of tobacco, please." Both Jenny and

the shopkeeper heard a sharp intake of breath from behind them. He saw a frown cross her face at the sound. Thomas Williams was fairly sure it came from Sally Adams, but like Jenny, he chose to ignore it. He nodded to Jenny, knowing exactly what sort she wanted without her having to ask. It was for the young sergeant without a doubt. It was the first time she'd bought tobacco in his shop. It couldn't be for anyone else.

Her items packed and paid for, Jenny gave Thomas Williams a grateful but somehow sorrowful smile. He walked around the counter and unusually held the shop door open for her, returning her smile as she passed through. As soon as the door was once more closed, the women gathered in the shop once more began whispering loudly among themselves. The shopkeeper, indignant with anger, nevertheless maintained his silence, and returned to tidying his shelves.

Outside, Jenny, shaking a little with both embarrassment and anger at the village women, waited a few moments for approaching tears to die away and gathered her thoughts together before mounting her bicycle and deliberately riding slowly and calmly away past the shop window, where she knew people would be watching. The atmosphere in the shop had been uncomfortable and almost icy and although nothing had been said, particularly to her, she knew instinctively that she was the cause of that silence. Thank goodness for Mr. Williams, she thought. She'd heard the level of conversation go back up soon after Mr. Williams closed the door of the shop behind her and it was that last thought that finally brought on the tears which she thought she'd managed to fight back. They were misting up her eyes as she crossed the bridge out of the village, now pedalling furiously to get away.

Jenny and the shopkeeper were not the only ones angry and upset over the incident and the gossip in the village. Martha Carter went into the shop shortly afterwards and managed to wheedle out of an irate Mr. Williams the reason for his anger, all of the other women having left. Joshua found himself on the receiving end of Martha's temper on her return to The Lamb.

"We did tell him there'd be talk," he said, attempting to calm her. He knew immediately from the look on his wife's face that what he'd said was yet again something he shouldn't have. "Oh, you know what I mean, Martha," he added, almost despairingly.

"Yes, we did tell him Joshua, and he chose not to listen, but that's not the point," she said sharply.

"Well what is? If he wouldn't listen to us, what can do?" said Joshua.

"We still have to try to help him," said Martha.

"How can we do that?"

"Well, you're in a good position behind that bar of yours to do something about it, aren't you?" She was right, of course, as usual; Joshua knew that. A pub was as much of a hive of gossip as anywhere else, even if it was mainly male-oriented gossip and looked at from a completely different viewpoint. It was a place for the men, over a few drinks, to put the world to rights, and to share opinions and ideas, and of course village gossip. Joshua, as landlord, acted as unofficial chairman of all these discussions, keeping order when necessary.

"It's bit different in the bar..." Joshua began, but seeing the look on his wife's face, stopped immediately.

"Why?" she asked coolly, her eyes fixed on his, which always made him feel uncomfortable.

"I can't tell people what to talk about or how to think," he said. "I'll lose my customers if I throw my opinion around too much." Martha gave him what he could only call a knowing look.

"All I'm asking is that you make sure that people know what you think about it all. Nathan's a good young man. It's the least you can do for him. And where else would they go to drink?"

Joshua walked thoughtfully out to the bar to open the pub, Martha's words ringing in his ears. She was right, as always, he thought. He was well aware, and knew that Martha was as well, that the men of the village had a completely different view of whatever night be happening at Smallbrook Farm to that of their womenfolk. It was an attitude that the women might suspect but which would never be admitted to, as some things were best left unsaid. The landlord permitted himself a smile as he undid the bolts on the main door, which was so rarely locked during the day. He pulled the doors open but was not surprised that there was no one there yet; it was still a little too early in the evening for some of his most regular customers.

As men started to drift in a little later, Joshua noticed sadly, not for the first time and certainly not for the last, that they were all older like himself. A whole generation was missing, not only from the pub, but from the village, the surrounding area and the country as a whole. Sons, nephews, and in some cases, grandsons, all had been kitted out in khaki and sent off to fight in France. All the talk at first was of their work and of what news they'd heard or read of how the War was going and some talk was still of the tragic loss that had shocked the country of Lord Kitchener on his way to Russia in HMS Hampshire. Joshua was kept busy pulling pints. Then one of them, Bert Adams, said that his wife Sally had seen 'that young Jenny Tiley' in the village shop earlier that afternoon.

"Walked in as bold as brass, she said she did," he finished. The other men started to chip in with their own wives' and daughters' opinions, most of which were to the detriment of Jenny Tiley. Nathan wasn't mentioned much, Joshua noticed.

"I think the women-folk are being a bit hard on the poor girl," he said loudly, taking a large gulp from the pint he'd poured for himself. A few of the men looked at him. "Well, it must be difficult running that farm, small as it is, on her own," he continued.

"Well, she's certainly not on her own," said Bert Adams to loud laughter.

"I think the girl's done a good job since old Harry had to give up helping her to look after his wife. And I'm glad that young man Holt is kind-hearted enough to give her a hand now." This was Thomas Williams, the shopkeeper, not one of Joshua's regular customers. He only occasionally popped for a half after closing the shop.

"And she does need the help out on that farm," agreed Harry himself, in for an evening pint while a neighbour watched his wife for him. "It's a kind thing for him to do. Me and the missus felt bad letting the poor girl down by not being able to help. It's taken a weight off my mind him being there, I can tell you."

"He's got himself a nice cosy spot there, though," argued Bert Adams, a man who'd never had a strongly held opinion in his life unless his wife Sally had told him what it was first.

"Any one of us would like to be in that young man's place," said old Arnold Turney, a man in his eighties and possibly Joshua's oldest customer, a man who could remember the old Queen's coronation when he was a young boy. "I know I would if I was younger, she's a pretty thing," he added with a twinkle in his eye. One or two of the men smiled at this, while others, including Joshua, laughed along with him. It was plain to see what was going through their minds, Joshua thought, but as the conversation continued back and forth, he was pleased to find that most of the men were glad to see Jenny Tiley getting some help from Nathan, but it was also easy to guess what they would all think if they knew Nathan was not being paid for his work. As if he could read Joshua's mind, Bert Adams doggedly continued his argument.

"It beats me how the girl can afford to pay anybody. There's no spare money to be made out at Smallbrook." Much to Joshua's relief that steered the conversation safely away from Jenny and Nathan and led to the men to a much more frequent topic of bemoaning the fact that there was no money to be made anywhere in the area, unless your name, as they all agreed, was George Wilkins.

Chapter Fifteen

Idle gossip was something Reverend Simpkins never allowed himself to become involved in. It was something he vehemently disapproved of - as far as his placid disposition would allow him to become vehement about anything. Yet it was something that had begun to plague both him and his parishioners recently and as a result it was very much on his mind as he strolled out of the village, enjoying the sunshine.

Reverend Simpkins was a quiet middle aged man, a bachelor firmly set in his ways, never having felt any urge to marry or raise a family, prepared whenever possible to go along with the flow of country life as God ordained it, as suited the parish of which he was proud to be vicar. A forgiving Christian, he was slow to anger and could always see both sides of an argument, but wouldn't stand for anything he considered to be injustice. There was never any "fire and brimstone" in his Sunday morning sermons, which were instead homely and persuasive arguments attempting to guide people he already considered intrinsically good further on down the road to their salvation. Pleas to "love one another", to be good neighbours and to be 'Good Samaritans' and always offer help where help was needed were often heard from his pulpit, but they were axioms almost taken very much for granted by his down to earth country folk of his flock, because that was the way they generally lived.

God for Reverend Simpkins was a benevolent forgiving God, all powerful and ready to help anybody in need who turned to him and the good reverend did his best to help his parishioners to follow this divine example. An important part of the Reverend Simpkins' duties, in his eyes, was visiting his parishioners regularly and he tried hard to ensure that none were left out, whether they were regular church goers or not. He wrote letters for villagers unable to do so for themselves, helped them with their problems and comforted them in their times of need, an all too frequent occurrence because of the war in France.

Peace and solitude were important to the Reverend, and he was one of those lucky people who never found that time dragged for them. He always had plenty to do, and if there were no parishioners to visit, and no sermon to write, there were always his books, being a keen and avid reader.

This particular sunny afternoon, it was the turn of Nathan Holt and Jenny Tiley at Smallbrook Farm to receive a visit and it was thoughts of how to help and provide guidance and advice that were uppermost in his mind as he approached the farmyard. He found Nathan sitting on a bench, stretched comfortably in the sunshine, leaning back against the milking shed wall. Nathan had a good view across both the farmyard and down towards the stream, and waved a friendly greeting as the vicar walked towards him, then rose and held out his hand.

"Nathan Holt, vicar. Pleased to meet you."

"Reverend Simpkins, vicar of this lovely parish," replied the vicar, immediately taken with the young man's friendly attitude.

"It's a glorious afternoon, Mr Holt."

"It is, Reverend Simpkins, but call me Nathan. Won't you take a seat and join me?" Nathan gestured towards the bench, surprised to see the vicar at the farm. As the older man settled himself to the bench, Nathan asked "Will you join me in a cool drink?" Nathan was enjoying a mug of cider. The orchard behind the farmhouse, small though it was, was big enough to produce a reasonable crop of apples, and Jenny, like many farmer's wives, used them to make her own cider.

"Mm, I rather think I will, but only lemonade if there is some. Some of my flock would certainly not approve of my drinking cider in the middle of the afternoon." His face broke into a big grin as Nathan glanced guiltily at his own half empty mug, and he continued "but if I was in your shoes, my boy, I would be sure to enjoy it." Nathan smiled and called across the yard to Jenny, who quickly brought a pitcher of lemonade and two mugs. She poured drinks for the vicar and herself and leaned casually against the door-frame of the milking parlour waving away efforts by both men to give up their seats for her. She was flushed from the heat of her kitchen and the usual few wayward strands of hair hung over her forehead, having escaped from the scarf she'd used to tie her hair back. Nathan couldn't help thinking once again how beautiful she looked and smiled at her, a smile she returned a little sheepishly, aware of the Reverend's presence. Their smiles did not go unnoticed.

"I came to the parish of Dalton Combe after you'd left Nathan," the vicar began, "but I knew your aunt and uncle. Lovely people and a sad loss to both to you and the village."

"Thank you, vicar. I noticed how well looked after their grave is."

"That'll be Harry Mason. He cares for the graveyard for us," replied the vicar.

"Harry?" laughed Nathan. "He seems to be having quite an impact on my life!" The vicar looked slightly confused, but before Nathan could explain, Jenny spoke.

"It's a surprise to see you, Vicar," Jenny said, thinking unhappily that despite the pleasantries there must be a reason for his visit, and that she probably already knew what it was.

"I was out for a stroll in the sunshine, and I happened to be coming this way, so I thought I would say hello. It's the duty of a shepherd to look after his flock, you know," he said, still with a big smile on his face. Nathan could see why he was so well liked by the villagers. "I find that I don't have time to see everybody as often as I would like, and I was worried that I may have neglected you of late, Mrs Tiley. Unfortunately, there are those in the parish who make great demands on my time."

"Please, Vicar, you've known me some time, call me Jenny. Calling me Mrs Tiley makes me feel so old!" This comment was rewarded with a smile from the Vicar.

"You say you were just passing, Vicar?" Nathan asked.

"Well, yes and no. I can't lie to you, it just doesn't go with the job you know." He laughed at his own humour, and was relieved to see Jenny and Nathan smile. "It's a strange situation, Nathan. May I address you frankly?" Nathan nodded. "It's about your relationship with Mrs. Tiley." Despite the Vicar's best efforts, Nathan couldn't help but notice the emphasis on the phrase 'Mrs Tiley'. Jenny noticed as well, and scowled.

"Let me put your mind at rest, Reverend Simpkins." Nathan's tone was noticeably cooler, a fact which didn't escape the vicar. "There's nothing going on at Smallbrook for anyone in the village to worry about. I help Jenny run this farm, and yes I do have a room here, separately from where Jenny sleeps." Outwardly calm, Nathan was deeply irritated inside, and knew that Jenny would be embarrassed by this conversation. Jenny however was more surprised at Nathan lying to the vicar, a man of God, presumably to preserve her reputation and hoped that the sudden flush on her face would be taken by the vicar as discomfort at the subject being discussed.

"I'm sure everything is respectable, Nathan, but I have a responsibility to all my parishioners, including Jenny and yourself, as you are so recently returned from..." His voice faltered uncomfortably.

"From Hell, Reverend?" Nathan prompted and was pleased to see the Vicar smile.

"Quite," said Reverend Simpkins. "but I was thinking France." His serious look returned. "Mrs Tiley, Jenny, I mean, is a widow, a vulnerable woman alone in our community, and I feel it my duty to share my concerns."

"Vicar, as you probably well know, Jenny is a very strong minded and independent woman. She simply needs a strong pair of arms around the place, and I am, as I'm sure you know, available and willing to help at the moment – without taking advantage of a vulnerable woman, as you put it."

Reverend Simpkins held up both his hands placatingly and gave both Jenny and Nathan what he hoped was a disarming smile. Jenny, however was feeling a little piqued at having the two men talk about her like this.

"Do either of you mind if I say something?" she asked. Both men looked at her, but she directed her comments to the vicar. "Nathan has been a tremendous help, vicar, but there's more. He's a good man and he's helping me, well, helping me get better..." Her voice tailed off into silence.

"Please, Jenny, Nathan, I haven't come here to preach a sermon or to lecture you. It's just a gentle word in your ears, out of concern. There are always people in a community who will look for immorality where there is none, and I'm afraid certain members of my flock are more fervent in that area than others." He smiled again.

"You mean people are talking about what they think is going on here?" asked Nathan. Reverend Simpkins made no reply, which was an answer in itself. He felt comfortable in the company of these two young people. They were a couple, or soon would be; he was convinced of that, but his experienced eye could detect nothing that could possibly be considered sinful about them. They were happy with each other's company and he felt that God could ask for nothing more. Both he and Nathan took generous gulps of their cold drinks.

"I've not seen you in church since you came back to the village." The remark was addressed to Nathan.

"I think I lost my belief in God in the trenches, vicar," Nathan said honestly. "I saw more pain and suffering than a loving and forgiving God could possibly allow. We believe God is on our side, and the Germans believe that he is on theirs. It doesn't make sense to attend church parades where you can hear the screams of wounded men and the chaplain is telling us God is good."

"It's a common saying that God moves in mysterious ways," said Reverend Simpkins. He was of the same opinion as Nathan. For the vicar, God was a God of happiness and love, not sorrow and suffering. The war was the devil's work, not God's.

"His ways are just a little too mysterious for me," said Nathan. "Particularly after what I've been through." The vicar nodded. He understood the young man's attitude.

"And what of you, Jenny?" As she hesitated to answer, he continued. "I know we've spoken of this before, but has your mind changed?" Jenny shook her head.

"I'm not ready for church yet, vicar. Life seems better every day, and I promise I will return to your flock soon." She gave him a heartwarming smile.

"Oh but you are part of my flock, church attendance or not," he said to her. "Both of you are. I'm always there if you need me. The vicarage door is always open, and God's house always welcomes visitors." He finished his drink and stood up. "Thank you for the drink, Jenny," he said, and turning towards Nathan, added "I hope to see both of you again soon." Neither Jenny or

Nathan spoke as the vicar left the farmyard and made his way down the lane.

"He would really like us to go to church, wouldn't he? Nathan asked, a smile on his face when the vicar had disappeared from view.

"Yes he would," agreed Jenny, but more seriously. Nathan noticed the seriousness in her tone and it made him think a little. Later, in the kitchen, he broached the subject again. Jenny didn't seem very happy to talk about it at first.

"Before Edward joined the army and went to France, we used to go to church every Sunday. It was something I insisted upon, and after he left, I carried on attending the morning service. When the telegram arrived..." Her voice tailed off a little, and he put his hand on hers for a little support. "Well, there didn't seem much point," she finished.

"I've never been much of a church-goer since I left Dalton Combe," Nathan admitted apologetically. "Church parade in the army like I told the vicar, but there's no choice in that." He stopped, looking at her. "If you feel ready to go to church, then I'll go with you." Jenny smiled in return, hoping that her concern did not show in her face. She still had not mentioned what had happened in the shop, as she hated being talked about and didn't want to share her worries with Nathan. "We could go this Sunday – if you want to," Nathan said and Jenny felt a moment of panic.

"But if people have been talking about us..." she began, but he interrupted gently.

"Jenny, we've nothing to hide from anybody. We've done nothing wrong and I would be proud to walk to church with you."

"But people always think the worst," she insisted.

"They do, I know, but it's what we think that is important," Nathan replied. Jenny didn't look or feel convinced. "Jenny, you're a respectable widow, and I immediately have a bad reputation because I'm a soldier, and everyone knows what soldiers are like, but no matter what other people think, I'm lucky to have you in my life." Both of them were aware of the issues they were skirting around, and Jenny began to feel a little embarrassed by Nathan's apparent openness. Then he rose from his chair with a big confident smile. "Church this Sunday, and that's an order, Mrs Tiley," he said, standing behind her, hands on her shoulders and kissing the top of her head.

Chapter Sixteen

Jenny's hat was lying on the kitchen table, white and summery with a piece of lacy net around it, and Nathan's uniform cap suddenly seemed very masculine to him when he tossed it onto the table alongside. Both were a little different from the hat he'd been wearing just six months earlier. "Tin hats" they called them. The steel helmets had saved many a man's life, but like so many of the other men, Nathan had intensely disliked wearing his. He sat down at the table to wait for Jenny and took a few deep breaths. The memories were still too fresh.

"I shan't be long, Nathan!" Jenny called out from upstairs. She sounded nervous; Sunday morning seemed to have come around very quickly.

"We've plenty of time", he called back, and settled more comfortably into his chair. The morning service at St Matthew's was not due to start until ten o'clock and there was enough time for them not to have to hurry. The church bells hadn't even started ringing yet to summon people to their worship. He understood her nerves; he was a little nervous himself about the reaction of some of the villagers to his escorting Jenny to church, but he could deal with that; it was Jenny he was worried about.

As they reached the wooden lych-gate into the church-yard, the bells were ringing out loud and clear over the village and the surrounding countryside calling the people to worship. On Sunday mornings, the church came into its own, fulfilling the purpose for which it was built. It was an old church, built by the

Normans, some said. Its stonework, weathered and worn over the centuries, had been dug from quarries on the Devon coast and worked by local masons. The church was a part of the landscape, its lofty spire visible over the entire vale, while the churchyard was as old as the church itself, a path leading to the church door weaving through the gravestones and shaded by ancient monkey puzzle trees.

Martha and Joshua were among the villagers gathered in small groups talking quietly as Nathan, impressive in his uniform, and Jenny, in her Sunday best, approached the church. Some turned and watched as Nathan protectively took Jenny's arm and Martha made no pretense of hiding her anger as she heard some muttered comments about the couple.

"It's disgraceful," she heard one voice whisper. "And her husband not long dead in his grave, killed fighting for his country."

"No respect for the church either," said another.

"They ought to be ashamed of themselves," added a third, a voice she recognised this time, Sally Adams. Joshua heard the comments as well and realised from the rising colour in Jenny's cheeks that she had too. The landlord hoped that none of the people whispering would have the stupidity, although they would probably have termed it moral courage, to say such things directly to the young couple. It angered him that these same women hadn't much liked Edward Tiley when he was alive. He stretched out his hand in greeting to Nathan and felt the young man's tension; as Martha reassuringly put her hand on Jenny's arm, he felt his sometimes fiery wife stiffen next to him as something else was said that he hadn't quite heard. Joshua had no doubt she was preparing for battle. He slipped his arm through hers.

"Now's not the time or the place Martha," he whispered into her ear, stepping in front of her towards the church door. Arm in arm with him as she was, Martha had no choice but to go with him. Her heart sank as she realised through her anger that he was right, but she consoled herself with an angry glare in the direction of the offending women. Taking Joshua's lead, Nathan guided Jenny after the landlord and his wife, stepping aside to allow her to go through the doorway first. He felt proud for her as she walked in head held high, knowing how important this was for her. As they walked down the aisle to a pew, there were friendly smiles from George Wilkins and his wife, the shopkeeper Mr Williams, Harry Mason and others. Nathan received a particularly warm welcome from John Evans and his family, with young Jack being very interested in Nathan's uniform. Martha and Joshua made space for them to sit in the pew alongside them. As he entered to begin the service, the Reverend Simpkins was pleased to see Jenny and Nathan sitting in the congregation.

If anyone had asked him, Joshua wouldn't have described himself as an ardent church-goer. He always attended service on a Sunday morning, but more from a self-conscious sense of duty, because it was what you were supposed to do, than from anything else. Anyway, Martha insisted. He followed the routine of the service, a hymn singing and prayers, a routine established by centuries of tradition, almost without thinking, much like many of the other villagers, he suspected. He sang lustily, particularly in the hymns he liked and stood, sat and knelt down where necessary. Being a tall man, the kneeling part was proving more and more difficult as the years passed. But his ears pricked up as he heard the Reverend Simpkins speak.

The vicar was not a great sermoniser, a fact for which the villagers were grateful, but usually by the time the collection was taken by the churchwardens, one or two thoughts were turning towards their Sunday dinners. Today looked like being a little different.

"I am not preaching a sermon today," the vicar began. "Instead, I would like to give you a short passage from the Gospel according to Saint Matthew, a little homely advice." He paused, having hopefully gained the attention of his congregation. His voice rose as he began again, carrying clearly throughout the old building. "'Judge not, that you be not judged. For with the judgement you pronounce you will be judged and with the measure you use it will be measured to you,' Matthew tells us. He goes on to say that it's all too easy for us to recognise what they think to be faults in other people without seeing the faults in ourselves. There is something I would like to add," the vicar said, almost as an afterthought. "'He that is without sin among you, let him cast the first stone' says St John." There was a lengthy almost uncomfortable silence while the vicar looked out over the congregation from his pulpit. Then he announced the next hymn.

With the ancient organ wheezing into life and the congregation rising to their feet, the rather strange mood created by the vicar's words dissipated and they all sang enthusiastically,

Reverend Simpkins leading them loudly. With the end of the hymn, George Wilkins rose to read the lesson, an unintelligible passage taken from the Old Testament book of Kings.

At the end of the service, the vicar waited in the porch by the church door, talking to his parishioners, a few words to each person as they left the building. He grasped Jenny's hand as she reached him, a large friendly smile on his face.

"It's good to see you here with us again, Mrs Tiley," he said, following it up quickly when he noticed her raised eyebrows, "I mean Jenny." His voice was loud enough to be heard by several nearby parishioners, who were looking in their direction. He put his hand on Nathan's shoulder. "Thank you for joining us, Sergeant Holt," he said, emphasizing Nathan's rank.

"Thank you for the service, vicar. It meant a lot to me to be here," Jenny said quietly.

"God is here for everyone," the vicar said even more loudly, a smile on his face which on anyone else Jenny would have described as almost wicked. She said as much to Nathan, Joshua and Martha as they all walked away.

"He was certainly making a point," Nathan agreed, with a smile.

Chapter Seventeen

It seemed to Nathan and Jenny that the days flowed by far too quickly. There seemed to be no end to the work to be done on the small farm but despite both of them always being tired, they could still find the time and energy to express their growing love for each other in the most natural way possible. Life was good for both of them and there appeared to be no clouds on the horizon to spoil their pleasure in each other's company. Even the village gossip seemed to have died down.

As for Nathan, he was thoroughly enjoying life at Smallbrook; the exercise suited him and seemed to be doing him good. Nightmares which had plagued him seemed to be a thing of the past, he was fitter than he had been for some time and although his left leg was still much weaker than the right and still dragging as he walked, it was stronger than it had been. The doctors had told him that it would be a long, long time before it would be better, If ever, and he had schooled himself not to worry about it. It would have been far worse had he lost the leg. All in all, Nathan felt that life was good.

Jenny was happy and aware that she was happy. For her, life over the last year had been a struggle, both with the farm and with her emotions. Edward had been the love of her life, the only man she had ever known really well, and although he'd had his faults she'd been devastated at the news of his death. Nathan had brought a breath of fresh air into her life and given her hope and confidence. In return she had given herself, heart body and soul.

Autumn had come around while they were wrapped up in their feelings for each other. The evenings were beginning to draw in and grow chilly, leaving less time for outdoor tasks. The new season had also brought with it an extra job and one Jenny enjoyed: the apple harvest. Cider season was upon them and the first step was for the ripe apples to be picked in Jenny's small orchard, an orchard of which she was both proud and protective. Nathan had asked her why. To him, although he refrained from saying so, one orchard was very much like another, despite knowing that different ciders had different tastes.

"Sleeping Beauty," she replied, a big smile on her face. Before Nathan could give her more than a curious glance at this strange reply, she carried on. "That's the name of the apple, 'Sleeping Beauty.' It's the only orchard in the area that has them and they make a lovely cider. One of the previous tenants of Smallbrook had the trees brought down from Worcester or Hereford way, where they're more common. Mr Wilkins always has a barrel of the cider they make." Jenny was happy to show off her knowledge, causing Nathan to smile at her enthusiasm.

"The best cider is made from orchards where there's only a single type of apple, and no intruders," she continued.

"Intruders?" asked Nathan.

"Intruders are just different types of apple," she explained, "and there are no intruders in this orchard." She sounded proud.

Before Nathan and Jenny could begin work in the orchard, there was the slight problem of the pigs and the geese, who had free roam of the area. With fresh fruit lying around, the pigs in particular couldn't be given access to the orchard and they were soon shooed back into the farmyard and the gate closed on them. The geese were a different matter. Trying to shepherd them away from the apple trees and back into the farmyard proved much more difficult. Finally, after much running around and arm waving and wing flapping in the case of the geese, Nathan and Jenny achieved their aims and corralled the reluctant birds in the farmyard. Holding tightly onto Nathan, Jenny could hardly move for a few minutes through laughing so much.

However fit he may have felt, Nathan found a whole new set of muscles aching when he began working in the orchard. To pull the ripe fruit from the trees, he used a long pole with a hook at one end, and firmly pulled the apple loose, letting it fall to the ground. Jenny gathered the picked fruit into piles, where they would be left until the cider-maker arrived with his mobile press in a few weeks.

They were over half-way through the orchard and thinking of a short break when Jenny heard the tinkling of a bicycle bell along the lane.

"I'll go," Jenny said, "and then I'll bring a drink back." leaving Nathan to it, she went back to the farmyard, where there was no-one in sight yet. Thinking to herself that the sound must have come further away than she'd thought she experienced a strange feeling of déjà vu when young Johnny Williams cycled breathlessly into the farmyard. Her stomach lurched.

"Telegram for you, Missus Tiley," he called out loudly. A telegram? She thought to herself. Who could possibly be sending her a telegram? Johnny quickly handed her the message and was off down the lane before she could offer him a glass of lemonade. He remembered what had been in the last telegram he'd delivered to Smallbrook. Jenny just stood in the farmyard staring at the envelope in her hand.

"Did I hear voices?" Nathan called from the orchard gate.

"It was Johnny Williams from the village," Jenny called back. "He's brought a telegram".

"Who for? Me or you?" Thoughts about being contacted by the army had begun to prey on his mind in the last few days. It was something that was inevitable, but that he hoped would be delayed for as long as possible.

"It's for me," she said. "But I don't want to open it." By now, Nathan had joined her in the farmyard. He put his arm around her shoulder.

"Why not? The last one you had was probably the worst news you could have. This one can hardly be as bad as that."

"I don't know, Nathan. It scares me and I don't know why." She paused and put the telegram in her pocket. "I'll open it later." She disengaged herself from his arm and walked towards the farmhouse. Nathan returned to the orchard, slowly shaking his head.

When he walked into the farmhouse kitchen later, he knew immediately that something was wrong. Jenny, sitting at the old table facing the door, had obviously been crying. The telegram was lying crumpled on the table in front of her.

"What's wrong?" he asked, pulling out a chair and sitting down. She didn't answer, lost in her own thoughts and oblivious to the question. "Jenny, what's wrong?"

"It's Edward. He's alive," she said not looking at him. Her voice sounded flat and drained of emotion.

"Where?" Nathan asked. Instead of replying she picked up the telegram and read it to him.

"Lieutenant Edward Tiley alive. Stop. In Hereford General Infirmary. Stop. Doctor Dougall." Her voice faltered again and she threw the telegram back on the table. Eddie alive! Her emotions were in turmoil, and she couldn't bring herself to look at Nathan, who sat watching her, a concerned look on his face, saying nothing, but taking her hands in his.

"Is that all it says?" he asked finally.

"Yes. I don't know what to do." She paused, thinking about what she'd just said. "No, I should go and see him, Nathan." Jenny was now in tears again. "He's alive and he's my husband". He nodded in agreement. They both sat in silence for minutes that seemed like hours.

"When are you going?" Nathan asked eventually.

"As soon as I can, but it's such a long journey. I don't know how I'll get there."

"You'll have to go on the train," he said after another long pause. "There's no other way. I'll look after the farm."

"Train? How will I ever afford that?" she asked incredulously.

"I'll pay for it."

"You? Why should you pay for me to go to see my husband, Nathan? That doesn't make any sense." She sounded surprised.

Chapter Eighteen

Jenny stepped onto the platform at Hereford railway station with a sense of relief, clutching her large bag close to her. She hadn't enjoyed the journey, although for the most part she'd had a third class compartment to herself. She'd been nervous about changing trains at Exeter and at the huge Temple Meads station in Bristol, where she'd come close to panic about not catching the right train and for almost four hours as the trains had made their gentle way across the countryside, she'd been alone with her thoughts, her mind in turmoil. She was glad to have arrived. She had nowhere to stay, but felt she had to get to the hospital and see Edward before doing anything else. She was here, and it would no good to put it off. A porter noticed her standing near the platform exit deep in thought.

"Anything I can do to help, Miss? You look a bit lost."

"Yes, please, thank you," she said. "I've never here before, and I need to get to the General Hospital," she continued, responding to his friendly tone. She relaxed her tight grip on her bag and placed it on the platform.

"The Hospital? You going to be a nurse, then?"

"No, no. My husband's there." It was strange saying the words. "I've come to see him. He was wounded in France."

"Oh, I'm sorry to hear that. I hope he's not too bad. We have 'em come through here, you know, before the Red Cross takes 'em off to the hospitals. Some of 'em's in a really sorry state."

"I'd been told he was dead," Jenny blurted out, not knowing why she said it. The porter looked sympathetic and put his hand on her shoulder.

"Then I'm sure he's going to be very glad to see you," he said encouragingly with a large smile. "Now let me show you which way to go. It should take you no more than twenty minutes and that only because you don't know the town." He took her bag for her and led her out to the main station entrance, where they stopped and he pointed her in the right direction, gave her some further instructions on where to go and left her with a cheerful "If you do lose your way, just ask someone. We're all friendly enough here and everyone knows where the Hospital is. Good luck – to you and your husband." She thanked him with a quick kiss on the cheek, and set off.

The walk through Hereford was pleasant enough, even though her mind was distracted. She walked along Commercial Road, lefts and rights and street names from the porter's directions already becoming mixed up. She remembered to turn at The Kerry Arms but thoughts of Edward continued to tumble over and over in her mind. She realised didn't even know how he had been wounded, or what injuries he had.

The railway porter's directions were very helpful, and after a couple more turns, she soon found herself in Nelson Street, underneath a large sign saying 'Hereford General Hospital' which was attached to a porter's lodge, where the porter smiled at her through the window. But she didn't go in. She couldn't. Not straight away.

Instead, she strolled up and down outside the lodge gates

for some time, pausing a little at the corner to look at the River Wye as it flowed past the hospital. She was unaware of the porter watching her curiously each time she came into view. Her anxiety at seeing Edward had increased with every step through Hereford and she'd almost convinced herself that she didn't want to see him at all. What was it going to be like? It had been two years. She had changed, and so would he. How had his injuries affected him? For that matter, what were his injuries? Would they be bad enough to shock her?

Thoughts of Nathan crowded in on her as well, adding to her mental confusion. She'd grieved for Edward, and had overcome her grief. She had fallen in love again. And now Edward was back, back from the dead, she thought. And the whole mess was not her fault. After all, the telegram had said starkly in black and white: 'Killed in action.' That left no room for any doubt.

She carried on walking up and down, people passing her by, going about their daily lives, doing their chores and errands, seemingly without a care in the world. Jenny felt like screaming. She had to go in. She knew that. She owed it to Edward. She'd married him, had declared that she would stand by him 'for better or worse, for richer for poorer, in sickness and in health, till death do us part.' But she'd been told that death had parted them and she'd cried, for night after lonely night, over the loss of her husband, all the time getting on with her life, as people had to, all over the country.

"Are you all right, Miss?" The porter, becoming worried, had finally come out of his lodge to see her. "It's just that you've been pacing up and down for almost an hour. You must be exhausted." He had the same warm inflection to his voice as the porter at the railway station. When he spoke, Jenny had stopped her pacing suddenly, causing a woman and a small boy to bump into her. She apologised to them, the woman muttering to the little boy as they walked off. Jenny then turned to the porter.

"Yes. Yes, I think so. I'm here to visit my husband."

"Very well, Miss. The main entrance is over that way," he said pointing to a large doorway in the impressive red-brick building. "Just as long as you're all right. Go in when you're ready." She thanked him and he returned to his lodge, but still kept an eye on her through the window.

After taking a number of deep breaths she walked slowly through the gate and across the yard, smiling at the porter as he passed his lodge, and went slowly up the steps to the massive portico sheltering the hospital entrance. Finally gathering herself together, Jenny decided that all her worrying was doing her no good. After all, she had travelled, how far was it the ticket-master at Exeter station had said? Yes, she had travelled something like one hundred and forty miles in uncomfortable trains and she wasn't going to waste that discomfort over a few worries.

The atmosphere of disinfectant and cleanliness was in complete contrast to the dusty roads outside, but most of all, it was the almost complete silence which Jenny noticed. She closed the heavy door and walked across to what appeared to be a reception desk of some sort, her shoes clattering on the polished tile floor.

"Can I help you?" a nurse in a finely starched uniform asked, looking up from filling in a form. She gave Jenny a welcoming smile that went some way to calming her nerves.

"Yes, my name is Mrs Jenny Tiley and I received this a few days ago," Jenny said, delving into her bag and pulling out the crumpled telegram that had told her Edward was still alive. The nurse read it quickly, and gave her another big, friendly smile.

"If you could sit over there for a few moments, Mrs Tiley," the nurse said, gesturing towards some uncomfortable looking chairs, "I'll inform Doctor Dougall that you are here." She turned away and walked through a door behind the desk, leaving Jenny to sit and wait.

It was a long wait and despite the chairs she must have dozed off, tired from her journey, because she was startled awake by a gentle hand on her shoulder and a voice speaking to her in a soft Welsh lilt.

"You'd be Mrs Tiley? I'm so sorry to wake you. Matron has asked me to take you upstairs to see Doctor Dougall and have a talk." The little nurse stood back slightly as Jenny got to her feet and led her to an office door on the first floor. She knocked and held the door open for Jenny to walk past her. A middle-aged man rose from his seat behind a large ancient looking oak desk completely clear of paper except for one official-looking file and gestured to an empty chair, which looked as uncomfortable as those downstairs. As Jenny sat down, the nurse closed the door behind her.

"My name is Dougall and I'm the doctor in charge of your

husband's case, Mrs Tiley. Matron here will be sitting in with us. Nothing happens in this hospital without Matron's say-so," he added, smiling. His voice was a velvety Scottish burr which immediately relaxed her. A stern looking woman nodded in Jenny's direction.

"Would you like a cup of tea and a biscuit?" The doctor asked. She nodded and answered she would. It had been a long journey and she realised she was very thirsty. She hadn't even thought of getting herself a drink.

"That would be lovely, thank you," she smiled. The Matron went to the door, stopped a passing nurse, gave her some instructions and returned to her seat. The doctor also resumed his seat then leaning forward slightly, rested his elbows on the desk's dark surface and formed his hands into a steeple shape, fingers touching his lips. He closed his eyes for a second and then looked at her.

"I thought you should know of your husband's injuries before you see him, Mrs Tiley," he eventually said.

"I don't know anything, not even how he was wounded, doctor. Until last week, I thought he was dead." She explained to him about the original telegram she'd received. He nodded sympathetically as she spoke.

"Unfortunately, because of the chaos of the war, this sort of thing does happen, more often than it should and I can do no more than apologise for the deficiencies of the War Department." He paused. "Let me assure you however, that your husband, Lieutenant Edward Tiley, is very much alive and in one of our downstairs wards. He has severe wounds caused by a shell blast, a direct hit on the trench he was in." Jenny felt her stomach churn. "But before continuing, I must ask you some questions, some of which may seem a little personal, for which I also apologise." He paused again, waiting for her agreement. She nodded, wondering what was coming, and noticing for the first time how tired the doctor looked. With a quick glance at the Matron, he began. "What was your husband like before the War?" The question took her a little by surprise.

"Before? I don't know really. I've never thought about it. He always enjoyed life, worked hard, always smiled, and was a very loving man." She felt almost embarrassed talking about her husband like this, and rather discomfited by the thoughts of Nathan that insisted on crossing her mind.

"How was his temper?"

"He could get angry over silly little things," she began and saw him nod slightly, as if he was hearing what he'd expected to. "But he never... he never hit me when he was angry, if that's what you were thinking," she added.

"He could be a very physical person, though?" the doctor enquired. She nodded again.

"Were you... were you, well, very close?" the doctor asked, slightly awkwardly.

"Close?" Jenny asked.

"Yes. Physically." She nodded, her increasing embarrassment suddenly preventing her speaking. "I'm sorry, Mrs Tiley, but these are questions I need to ask. Do you have

135

any children?" She shook her head. He nodded, as if registering the information, and then paused as a nurse knocked on the door and came in carrying a tray with tea and biscuits. Matron poured them all drinks and he let Jenny drink her tea and eat some biscuits and poured her a second cup, before speaking gently, a slight frown on his face.

"There are some things you need to know before you see your husband. His injuries are quite extensive." He paused. "Because of that, I feel you should be prepared for quite a shock. He's also suffered a lot in his mind and you may find him a very changed man from the one you knew." He looked apologetic as if it was all his fault. Jenny said nothing, waiting patiently for him to continue, a gnawing feeling of anxiety verging on panic growing within her.

"To start with his physical injuries. The shell blast caused a lot of damage to his right arm, which had to be amputated at the elbow, and to his legs, so much so that both have been amputated below the knee..."

"Both his legs?" She couldn't help but interrupt.

"Yes. He will need a wheeled chair to be even in the slightest bit mobile, and will of course always need help getting in and out of bed and getting to the toilet." He paused again, looking unwilling to continue. A nod from the Matron encouraged him. "But unfortunately there is more. When the shell exploded, he was thrown into a tangle of barbed wire." He noticed Jenny catch her breath and a look of shock cross her face. She closed her eyes for a few seconds before opening them once again. "This caused massive scarring to his chest and stomach, which is healing well, but will lead to the skin being slightly more inflexible than before. Also and how shall I put this, the wire caused severe damage to his, um, private parts. I'm sorry to say he will never be a father, nor will he be able to..." Jenny's embarrassment caused him to stop. She knew what he was about to say. She drank some more tea, obviously close to tears, and he waited for her to compose herself.

"Surely there can't be any more? Isn't that enough?" she asked quietly, almost in a whisper, gazing into her cup and avoiding eye contact with the doctor. He seemed acutely aware that she was talking more to herself than to him, but it was a question that nevertheless needed an answer. While trying to maintain a professional remoteness, he was beginning to feel for this poor young woman.

"I'm afraid there is, Mrs Tiley. I realise that this is an awful lot for you to take in, but you really do need to know everything before I can let you see him." She nodded, still unable to look at him, and asked him to continue.

"Unfortunately, he has also suffered bad injuries to his face." She groaned, unable to stop the noise. Eddie had been such a good-looking, handsome man.

"What sort of damage?" she asked, dreading the answer.

"He's lost an eye and an ear, both on the right, and there is extensive facial scarring, which has needed surgery, but again is healing well."

"Oh my God!" cried Jenny, her hand going to her mouth. "How is he, after all this?" she managed to ask after taking a few moments to gather herself, embarrassed at her own reaction. She had not expected his injuries to be so serious and so extensive.

"He is lucky to be alive, Mrs Tiley, but as I said, his mind has been affected. With all of his injuries, much of the time he wishes he was dead. At other times, he realises he's lucky, and seems happy and relaxed. But these moods do swing to and from each other. You will have to remember that he has suffered terribly." He looked at her carefully and smiled. "I know this has been an awful shock for you, but I think seeing you will do him good."

Jenny could do no more than nod and lower her head into her hands. Then the tears started, a trickle at first, and then an uncontrollable flood that wouldn't stop as she grieved for her husband for a second time.

Chapter Nineteen

Edward Tiley would have been very surprised had he known that Doctor Dougall thought that at times he felt lucky to be alive and seemed happy and relaxed. He didn't. He was far from being a happy man. He was angry, bitter and morose. It was just that on some days when he felt able to and most importantly inclined to, he could mask his true feelings. The regimented routine of the hospital annoyed him beyond words. When he wanted to be left alone, which was most of the time, there was always at least one nurse fussing around him, and when he did infrequently feel in need of a little company, he would see no one for hours. Damned place! The sooner he was out of here the better.

He was in a bed in the corner of a huge ward, with a high ceiling, a hard floor polished to perfection and massive windows which let in a lot of light and overlooked the river. The beds were well spaced out, slightly too far apart for the wounded soldiers to be able to talk to each other, a situation Edward was actually quite grateful for. There was only one military ward in the hospital, holding twenty two officers and enlisted men, while the rest of the hospital dealt with the civilian sick of Hereford.

The presence of the other ranks was another thorn in Edward Tiley's side. Since joining the army he had become very conscious of his position as a lieutenant, and had picked up the attitude from his fellow officers that the other ranks were inferior in status to him in every way. Added to that, he had run a farm, and was not just some farm labourer. It gave him some standing if not actually a boost when he joined the Yeomanry, and had enabled him to start his army life as a lieutenant. The county set were much more aware of status than ability, and Edward's lack of the latter had not endeared him to the men serving under his command.

He lay and looked at the seemingly far away ceiling, a familiar despairing feeling of helplessness starting to creep over him once more, a feeling which constantly fuelled his anger. Edward was all too aware that his life had changed irrevocably and forever, and the simple fact that no amount of determination, or stubbornness on his part was going to change it back and replace what he had lost angered him. But he was damned sure that he wasn't going to spend the rest of his life stuck in a hospital. Whatever it took. He was a fairly young man and although he knew he would have to be looked after, he was also certain that it would not be by these hatchet faced harridans in their starched uniforms, who seemed to treat him and all of their other patients as nothing more than lumps of meat.

What he wanted more than anything was to get back to Smallbrook. That idiot Scottish doctor had told him it was impractical and could never happen, but Edward wasn't having any of that. Smallbrook was where he wanted to go, and Smallbrook was where he was going. Jenny would look after him, he was sure of that.

He'd drifted off into a fitful sleep, which was how he spent most of his time, when he was woken by a gentle grip on his shoulder and the all too familiar sound of a gentle Scottish accent.

"Lieutenant Tiley, Edward, it's Doctor Dougall. You have a visitor". The soft Scottish burr eased him back into a dopey wakefulness.

"Hello Eddie," said a voice from his blind side. He recognised it immediately.

"Jen. You came," was all he could say, turning his head to look at her. She hadn't changed, looking exactly as the image he had carried in his head since enlisting. He said so. "You haven't changed. It's good to see you." His voice sounded the same as she remembered.

"It's good to see you, too, Eddie, and yes of course I came," replied Jenny. The doctor coughed politely and interrupted.

"I'll leave you two alone for a wee while, but even though you've lots to talk about, only a short visit this time." He turned and walked away from them, stopping to have a quiet word with the matron. A nurse was quickly with them, drawing curtains around the bed to give them a little privacy. Jenny sat on the edge of the bed and took Edward's hand in both hers, looking directly at him. She hoped she'd managed to hide the shock she'd felt on seeing him, a shock she'd been only marginally prepared for by Doctor Dougall. Despite the doctor's words, she'd felt something give way inside her when she saw him asleep in his bed. The handsome, almost god-like face she remembered was gone, the still fairly crude surgical procedures used to reconstruct his face having managed only to produce a cruel parody of a face, certainly not Eddie's. She didn't dare to think about the changes to his body, just forced herself to remember that whatever the injuries, he was still Eddie.

"You've been through a lot Eddie, so the doctor tells me," she said calmly. "They sent me a telegram and told me you were dead." Edward wasn't sure about her calling him Eddie. It didn't seem right. No one had called him anything but Edward or Lieutenant Tiley since he joined the Yeomanry, and that was how he now saw himself.

"I'd have been better off dead," he said without thinking of who he was talking to. Jenny, feeling a lurch in her stomach, almost recoiled from the bitterness in his voice. She quickly changed the subject to Smallbrook. They chatted about the farm for a short while, his mood improving, then he asked "How have you been managing, Jen? It must have been difficult while I've been away." It was a question she'd been expecting but not looking forward to. She explained how helpful George Wilkins, their landlord, had been and also about the help she'd had from Harry Mason and how much of a godsend he'd been, but how his wife was now ill and he couldn't come. He said very little, just listened, surprised at how she'd coped, but she noticed a different tension in him when she said there was somebody new helping her out now, an ex-soldier named Nathan Holt.

"Was he in the Yeomanry?" he asked. He didn't recognise the name.

"No," she said, realising that she didn't know much about Nathan's time in the army. He didn't talk about it much.

"Regular army, then," said Edward, helping her out a little.

"Yes, a sergeant. He was wounded at Ypres." Edward

chuckled, an unusual sound for him in this place.

"A sergeant. Then he'll do what a lieutenant tells him when I come back to Smallbrook, won't he?" The notion that Edward might want to come back to live at Smallbrook took Jenny completely by surprise. Not only had she not considered the possibility, the thought of what he was going to do for the rest of his life had not even occurred to her. She was still in shock from finding he was alive. She felt a sharp pang of guilt as that thought took hold. Unconsciously, learning of his injuries from Doctor Dougall, she must have assumed that he would need to stay in a hospital of some sort, if only because of the care he so obviously needed. The pang of guilt sharpened as she looked at him lying in the bed, waiting for her to speak.

"Have you talked to the doctors about this, Eddie?" she asked.

"Doctors? What do they know about what's good for me?" he snorted. "I'm the one who's got to live like this, Jen. If they had their way, I'd be shut up in some institution for the rest of my days. I can't stand that. I mean, you just look around this place." He sounded earnest. She was unable to give him an answer. She'd looked around when Doctor Dougall brought her into the ward. It was an unpleasant, soulless place, despite the best efforts of the nurses.

"How would you manage on a farm, Eddie? My time is all taken up now. How could I look after you? I wouldn't know what to do, I'm not a nurse."

"You're my wife, Jen," Eddie said flatly. "You'd manage, I

know you would." His voice became firmer, and he pulled his hand away from hers grabbed her arm. "In sickness and in health, and all that, remember?" She put her hand gently on his where it was gripping her.

"I don't know Eddie. This is all a shock to me. Only a week ago I thought you were dead. I'll have to talk to Doctor Dougall about what you might need and how we might be able to manage."

"What I need, Jen," he said abruptly, "is to be at home being looked after by you, my wife, and that is what is going to happen, no matter what any foolish Scottish doctor may have to say about it!" His voice had risen sharply.

"Eddie..." Jenny began, but Eddie interrupted.

"I said you're my wife, Jen. You'll do as you're told!" Jenny, surprised at his harsh tone, was about to answer, when she heard footsteps. The matron appeared through the curtains and stood by the side of the bed looking sternly down at her patient.

"Lieutenant Tiley, I have asked you before on a number of occasions to keep your voice down. It disturbs the other patients," she said, ignoring the look of anger on Edward's face. She turned to Jenny, speaking more gently and with a sympathetic smile. "Mrs Tiley, I'm afraid I'll have to ask you to leave. Doctor wanted this to be a short visit so as not to upset either of you too much." Jenny nodded and Edward scowled. She stood and leaned over him and kissed him on his scarred cheek. His hand went straight to the spot.

"I'm sorry," she said hurriedly. "Did that hurt?"

"No. Can't feel a thing," Edward said snappily. Jenny tried to ignore the thought that he sounded like a sulky child.

"I'll be in to see you again Eddie," she said, hoping for a response. There was none, just another scowl as she walked through the curtains and out into the ward. A number of the other patients were looking at her, and she had to fight back tears as she walked to the door. The matron followed her into the corridor.

"Is it possible for me to see Doctor Dougall again?" Jenny asked.

"He said for me to take you to him when you'd finished," the matron replied, and led her down the stairs and back to the doctor's office.

Chapter Twenty

Doctor Dougall looked up from the file in which he was writing as the matron knocked on his office and entered without waiting for an answer. He gave Jenny a welcoming smile and gestured for her to sit in the same chair she'd occupied only a little earlier, while the matron walked around to his side of the desk and whispered a few words in his ears. He nodded, a slightly resigned look on his face, before asking the matron to organise a pot of tea for him and his visitor. Then as the office door closed behind her he closed the file and settled back in his chair.

"A little frosty on the outside but a heart of gold," he said, obviously referring to the departed matron. Jenny didn't know whether to say anything having hardly met the woman and remained quiet. "How did you find your husband, Mrs Tiley?" he continued. She took her time answering, and he noticed tears in her eyes.

"He's changed so much," she said. "Even those few minutes, I could tell how much this affected him."

"He's been through more than we can possibly imagine," the doctor agreed. "I understand he mentioned going home to your farm," he added. "I should have said something before you saw him." Jenny looked at him with something close to reproach. "He's talked about it before, but I've tried to dissuade him. For someone with his level of injuries, a farm is totally unsuitable in my opinion. I fear it's the reason he asked me to contact you."

"It was Eddie's idea? Why now? Why did he wait?"

"He hasn't said, but I think he might have wanted to come home to you under his own steam as it were and that he asked me to contact you when it became very apparent that was not possible." Jenny felt furious.

"How long has he been here?" she asked. Doctor Dougall checked his file.

"Three months."

"Three months that I could have known he was still alive? Could you or the authorities not have told me?" Jenny had very quickly worked out that three months ago was about the time she'd first met Nathan. Had it really only been that long? Doctor Dougall said nothing, just turned the file around on his desk and gestured to the cover. She read where his finger indicated. 'Next of kin notified.'

"I'm sorry," he said. Jenny didn't know what to say. It certainly wasn't this apparently kind doctor's fault. The tea arrived and Matron once more did the honours before taking her former seat. After the slight pause, he continued. "Matron told me it sounded like you were having words with each other. I don't mean to pry, but I assume it was about him going home." Jenny nodded, clutching her steaming cup of tea.

"It's what he really wants," she said, trying to stand up a little for husband.

"But not you?"

"I hadn't thought of it until he told me," she admitted, knowing she should have prepared herself for the possibility, but she certainly wasn't going to admit to the doctor that the idea

148

frightened her. "I wouldn't know what to do, what he needed, but if it's what he really wants..." She took a sip of tea.

"Mmm, I take it he was a wee bit persistent?" Jenny nodded. "Did he tell you what he and I had talked about?"

"No, soon after he said about coming home, matron asked me to leave because he was getting upset. What was it?"

"Prosthetic limbs."

"Sorry?" She looked at him puzzled, not understanding.

"False arms or legs," the doctor explained. "There's a hospital at Roehampton near London, Queen Mary's, where they make new limbs for wounded soldiers. It was set up by a woman named Mary Eleanor Holford just last year. A wealthy woman, she'd apparently met a soldier who'd lost both his arms, and decided that anyone who had the misfortune to lose a limb in this awful war should have the opportunity to be fitted with the best artificial limbs that science could provide. They make the limbs in their own workshops." He stopped for a sip of tea and smiled sheepishly. "You'll have to forgive me, Mrs Tiley, but I think it's a marvellous project and ideal for soldiers like your husband."

"What did he think?" she asked, taken with the doctor's enthusiasm.

"He said no."

"Did he say why?"

"He was tired of hospitals and doctors and didn't want to spend any longer in hospital than he had to. Going to Queen Mary's would have needed a much longer stay."

"Just to have false legs and an arm made?" Jenny asked.

"It's not just the making of them. They would be specifically for him and the time is needed to teach the patients how to use their arms or legs properly. A lot of work in the gymnasiums and their workshops from what I can gather from my reading. The place is gaining a wonderful reputation for its success stories."

"But my husband's not interested." Even to herself, her voice sounded a little flat. She smiled a little to hopefully make up for it.

"No. I have tried to explain to him that if he had two new legs and crutches he would be able to get about better without having to depend on anybody else, because that is something else he becomes annoyed about. It would give him a little independence. I thought that might persuade him." He noticed her cup was empty. "Can I pour you another?" he asked.

"Yes please," she replied. "If he feels so strongly about it, is there any other way he could come back to the farm?"

"Without being bed-ridden? Only in a wheel chair, but they're not very stable on rough ground. They're really only suitable in towns or places where the grounds and paths are well-kept."

"Like a hospital," she said and then added "but it would be possible?"

"Yes, but..." his voice trailed off. "You've already said you wouldn't know what to do," he added lamely. A look of determination was appearing on her face replacing the worry and concern. It surprised him; it was if she was having a change of heart.

"It means a lot to Eddie," she said, "and as he pointed out a little while ago, I am his wife, and a wife has a duty to her husband." She paused as if gathering her thoughts and the doctor had the fleeting impression that she hadn't made up her mind – she was still trying to convince herself. "I'm not a nurse, would I be able to look after him properly?" Doctor Dougall looked down at the file on the desk and began enumerating things, ticking them off on his fingers.

"Firstly, he can't dress himself, although he can was and bathe himself if helped in and out of the bath and the bath prepared for him. He can shave but the new part of his face is unlikely to grow any facial hair. He can eat and feed himself, but can't prepare meals or cut up his own food." He had the sudden impression he was being brutal, while the woman sat opposite him was trying to be positive, or at least consider if she could help. However, he couldn't shake himself of the feeling that she should not be forced into a position where she had to devote the rest of her life to looking after a husband she'd thought was dead just because the man stubbornly refused to stay in hospitals. "As for the toilet, it's the nurses' secret weapon, the bedpan, which is unfortunately humiliating at the best of times." He paused. "Mrs Tiley all of this may sound harsh, but I'm trying to present you with a realistic picture of what you can expect and to make you realise how difficult all of this would be for you on a farm."

"But it could be done?" she asked. He nodded. "What about nursing care?" she added.

"He doesn't actually need any monitoring care, apart from occasional visits from his own doctor. Is there one in the village where you live?"

"Yes, Doctor Allerby, a very good one."

"Well his physical injuries are healed, but he will sometimes need something to keep pain at a bearable level. I would have to write to your doctor about that. Allerby, you said his name was?" He scribbled it down when Jenny nodded, and then looked up at her again. "As for his mind, that is a more difficult problem."

"Would being back at home help that?" she asked.

"Yes I think it would, but remember I'm not an expert in problems of the mind, Mrs Tiley. I would still find it hard to recommend him going home, as I'm not convinced it would be good for either of you, but the final decision rests with you and your husband." He still felt that Jenny was reluctant, although possibly resigned to doing what she saw as her duty and that she try to make the best of it. He wondered if there was any way he could make it easier for the couple. "There is no need to rush into a decision this afternoon, Mrs Tiley. I realise that this has all been a shock for you and you need time to think. Why don't you come and see me tomorrow morning at about eleven o'clock after my rounds and we'll have another talk. Should your husband go home with you, it would take some days to make the necessary arrangements anyway, so I assume you have somewhere to stay?"

"No, I hadn't thought of it. I was going to look for

somewhere when I'd finished here." She felt slightly foolish about her lack of arrangements, and then surprised as Doctor Dougall stood with a smile.

"There's an excellent lodging house not five minutes from the front door of the hospital," he said. "It's run by a Mrs Ferguson, a fellow Scot, and is very respectable as well as being reasonably priced. I stayed there myself when I first came South." He walked around the desk and held out his hand to help her up, before taking an overcoat from his coat-stand. "I'm only writing up patient's notes this afternoon, so I can walk you around and show you the way. If you wanted me to?" As she stood, he thought she looked tired, a woman in need of a little moral support. It also occurred to him that there might just be a little more on her mind than her husband returning to their farm.

Mrs Ferguson turned out to be a lovely welcoming woman who could best be described as grey-haired, small, round and motherly, only coming to Jenny's shoulder as she ushered her in through the front door. She was more than happy to find a homely and comfortable room for Jenny and provide a slice of home-made cake, a small glass of sherry and some company while she found out what brought Jenny to Hereford. Jenny then had a lie down for an hour or so before freshening up and changing out of her travelling clothes. She was nervous about joining the other guests for an early evening meal and kept herself to herself, joining in the conversation only when she couldn't avoid it without appearing impolite. After the meal, which she thoroughly enjoyed, having eaten little since setting out from Smallbrook, she excused herself from everyone's company, claiming tiredness after her long journey. Sleep, however, eluded her and it was silent tears that kept her company until the small hours of the morning when she finally drifted off.

Chapter Twenty-one

Jenny was later rising and consequently later for breakfast than the other residents and had the small dining room to herself. Mrs Ferguson, having grown up daughters of her own but all married and away, knew at one glance that Jenny was a troubled young woman this morning. She said nothing while cooking and serving her breakfast, but when Jenny had finished eating, she took her cup of tea and sat down with her. Jenny was happy of the company.

"Your husband being in hospital troubling you, my dear?" Mrs Ferguson asked. Jenny smiled.

"A little," she answered. She had a little difficulty with Mrs Ferguson's accent, which seemed much harsher than Doctor Dougall's and rather strange coming from this kindly person.

"Aye," the Scotswoman had told her the previous evening, "we're from different parts of Scotland, but both glad to be away." She'd then lapsed for a few seconds in a broad Scottish accent that Jenny had found totally indecipherable. This morning however, she was more understandable.

"You said he had bad injuries. Is that what's upsetting you and what kept you awake half the night? And if you think an old woman's being nosy, then tell me so." Jenny smiled again. Mrs Ferguson was easy to talk to. Could she tell her what was really troubling her?

"I just don't know how I'll manage to look after him," she said.

"Have you no help on that farm?" the older woman asked, and then seeing Jenny's cheeks flush, nodded with an understanding 'ah, you do have help then."

"Yes." Mrs Ferguson stretched out her hand to take Jenny's.

"You've done nothing wrong. You thought your husband dead."

"But now I know he's not," said Jenny.

"Well, my girl, when I've a troubled mind I take myself off to the cathedral – it's a grand place – and share my troubles with God. Most times He helps settle my mind. The peace and quiet will help you find your way."

As Doctor Dougall had asked Jenny to call into the hospital to see him at around eleven o'clock, Jenny had time to spare and putting on her hat and coat, she decided to take Mrs Ferguson's advice and visit Hereford Cathedral. She had never seen a cathedral, let alone been inside one. So, with Mrs Ferguson's words of "Take care, dear" ringing in her ears, she once more walked through the streets and lanes of the city, boldly asking for directions. Catching tantalising glimpses of the huge cathedral over rooftops and down alleyways, she didn't notice that anxious thoughts and worry about Eddie and Nathan were already being edged to one side of her mind because of the unfamiliarity of her surroundings. She remembered to turn left at the Lloyds Bank, which was in a lovely black and white building and walking further along High Town she saw the busy entrance to the Butter Market. Tempted for a few moments to go in, she instead turned the opposite way.

She came upon the cathedral on emerging from the narrow Church Street, facing an imposing porch and doorway across the cathedral close and just stopped. The sheer size of the building was something she'd never before experienced. It just seemed to reach up into the sky. She followed it up with her eyes and stood with her head tilted back, just staring.

"Reaching out to God," a deep voice said at her shoulder, "but you should really see it from the west front." She hadn't even been aware of anyone standing close to her and jumped a little. She tore her gaze away from the cathedral to look at the owner of the voice, surprised to see it was a young man. Too tall and thin for his own good, she thought immediately, someone who looked like he could do with a good meal. He was the possessor of the most untidy mop of black hair she'd ever seen and underneath was a pale, earnest looking face dominated by a pair of heavy looking spectacles. He was wearing a long black clergyman's robe which didn't quite hide a pair of scuffed boots. Seeing her jump a little, he said "I'm sorry. Did I startle you?"

"No, no," she said. "I was just looking at the cathedral."

"It's lovely, but you must let me take round to the west front. It's much more impressive," he offered. She had to admit, having accepted the invitation and gazing up at the high towers and the ornate decoration, that it was, as he'd said, 'much more impressive.' He pointed out the statues of various saints and notables from history, apologising for them being mostly worn and unrecognisable as if it was his own personal fault, then escorted her inside the building, explaining as he did so that he would have to leave her there. "There is always work to do for God," he said smiling. As he started to walk away, he paused and turned and with another smile, said "Pray to God. He will help you in your troubles." Then he was gone. Grateful for his brief companionship and the distraction it had brought, she realised that she didn't even know his name.

Taking a seat about halfway along the nave, she looked around and drank in the wonderful atmosphere of the building. Inside, even more than outside, her eye was drawn upwards; pillars and windows all seemed to point to the ceiling, as if to say 'Raise your eyes up to the glory of God.' Used to small churches as she was, Jenny was awed by the cathedral. Mrs Ferguson had been right about the place, so Jenny just sat and let her mind wander, and thought by thought, worry by worry, the problem of Eddie and Nathan returned. There were people around, as cathedrals have always been places of pilgrimage, but they seemed almost insignificant against the size of the building. They certainly didn't disturb her thoughts.

She'd made her mind up about what to do and knew she'd probably decided as soon as Eddie reminded her that she was his wife. She loved Nathan deeply; he had brought a light into her life, an explosion of love, warmth and deep feeling that Eddie never had. But her vows had been made before God. A tear rolled down her cheek and she dabbed it away with her handkerchief. The one thing she thought would never happen to her was that she would be a woman torn between two men. Another tear dabbed away. She knew she wouldn't be able to manage Eddie and the farm on her own, but would Nathan stay? Was it fair of her to even think of it? Things couldn't be the same between them, not with Eddie home. She loved Nathan too much send him away from her and too much to ask him to stay. Another tear appeared, quickly followed by another, until there was a steady stream of them on her cheeks to be dabbed at with the handkerchief. She needed Nathan to stay at Smallbrook, needed him there for her, but she couldn't refuse Eddie's demand to come home, couldn't condemn him to a lifetime of being in hospital just for her own happiness. It was the thought of hospital that steadied her. She had an appointment with Doctor Dougall and it was time to tell him of her decision.

Chapter Twenty-two

"My dearest Nathan," the letter began, and Nathan's heart soared as he read of Jenny's feelings for him, an outpouring written in a girlish hand with spelling mistakes and crossings out. As he read on, however, his mood sank as if dark clouds were covering the sun. Edward, although severely injured – Nathan found it difficult to understand how the man coped with having two legs and an arm missing – was coming back to Smallbrook. And Jenny was asking in the letter if he would make the necessary arrangements for his arrival.

He'd been happy over the last months with Jenny, a happiness that he'd not been able to find at any time during his adult life and he knew he'd do as she wished. Everything would be ready for her husband's return, but there was a part of him that wanted to leave, to not be here when she came back. He hadn't realised that happiness could be so elusive and could slip away so easily.

The work in the orchard was finished until the travelling press arrived, the apples were stacked neatly under the trees and covered in straw and sacking, and there were few other urgent chores that needed doing. Jenny had asked for a bed to moved downstairs into the kitchen. After doing that, Nathan made up a bed for himself in the hayloft. He would be unable to stay in the house, or with Jenny with Edward back.

George Wilkins was surprised at receiving a visit from Nathan and even more surprised at the news he brought.

"What in God's name does the man think he's doing?" he'd exclaimed. "How can he live on a farm with injuries like that?" Nevertheless he'd agreed to loan a wagon and a horse, and offered to drive it himself, to help Nathan out, but he was worried about the younger man. "What will you do, lad? Stay on at Smallbrook?"

"How can I with her husband home?" Nathan replied.

"He's not going to be able to help out much, is he? She's still going to need a strong pair of arms about the place." The old farmer put a hand on Nathan's shoulder. "Seeing you both week after week coming to church, it's as plain as the nose on your face what you both feel for each other. Are you really going to walk away from that? If you care for her, you'll stay and help." Nathan was uneasy talking about his feelings to the older man. Instead he told him he'd already made up a bed in the hayloft.

"I've slept in worse places," he said smiling. "It's better than a shell hole." Having managed a change of subject, he went to arrange times with George and then walked back to Smallbrook.

He'd thought the place was desolate and lifeless after Jenny had simply left for Hereford, but that was nothing compared to how he felt sitting in the empty kitchen with her letter once more in his hand, his back turned away from the bed and the curtain he'd put up to give Edward Tiley some privacy. Nathan knew without the shadow of a doubt that he had lost Jenny to her returning husband, and that he'd lost her because of her sense of duty, her sense of doing what was right after the unthinking storm of happiness they'd been caught up in.

162

Tired though he was, Nathan found it difficult to sleep. He'd decided to carry on sleeping in the house until Jenny and Edward returned; then would be the time to start roughing it in the barn. But the bed, as it had been on each of the nights she'd been away, was cold and lonely without Jenny lying beside him. He lay for what seemed like long hours, hands behind his head, staring at the bedroom ceiling.

The sound of the brook running past the open window, the brook that gave Smallbrook its name, also kept Nathan awake. Relaxing though the sound normally was, tonight he found it irritating. Its trickling seemed to mirror the bubbling flow of thoughts through his mind. What was he to do about Jenny? He knew that he'd fallen in love with her and needed to be with her, and she'd told him the same, even in the letter, but he also knew how confused she was about her husband. He cursed silently into the darkness, wishing that the man was as dead as Jenny had presumed he was, even though he didn't know him, then berated himself for having had the thought. The brook carried on trickling and bubbling, and his thoughts kept up their never ending circling in his mind but slowly and gradually he drifted off to sleep.

He became aware of a voice in the distance. It seemed of no concern to him and he tried to ignore it. Why would somebody be calling his name in the middle of the night?

"Sergeant Holt! Sergeant Holt!" the voice cried, but it was only when a hand firmly shook his shoulder that Nathan's sleep was finally shattered. He came awake instantly. It was a habit he, and many others, had acquired in the trenches of France.

"'Ere, sarge, there's a runner wants you". Nathan looked up into the face of his lance corporal, a young lad named Williams, whom nothing ever seemed to distress. Even now, in the deepest part of the night, he had an amiable, mischievous grin on his face. Nathan sat up, grateful that for once the rain had held off, although one dry night would do little to help the muddy squalor of the trenches.

"Let's have him in here, shall we?" he said only a little blearily. The messenger, when he came into the dugout from the trench, was still breathless.

"Message from Captain Urquahart for you Sergeant", he panted. He handed Nathan a sealed packet.

"All right, private, take a minute to catch your breath while I read this. There might be a reply." Nathan motioned towards the only chair in the dugout, onto which the man sank gratefully. Nathan remained seated on the edge of his cot. He tore open the sealed packet and began to read. Urquahart was his immediate superior, his own platoon officer having been killed the previous week. Nathan had been in nominal charge since. He swore under his breath when he read the contents. The Captain wanted a small patrol of men, three at the most, to go into no man's land and cut barbed wire prior to a minor push the following morning. There would be no reply to a direct order, so Nathan had Williams make the grateful messenger a cup of tea and went out into the trench. He quietly called for volunteers for the task and selected two men, intending to lead them himself.

What seemed like only moments later, he was looking out into no man's land through the trench periscope. The constant rain had turned the French countryside, war torn as it was, into a muddy stinking swamp. Nathan smiled grimly to himself in the darkness. Life in the trenches was a constant horror, but at least he was still alive to reflect on it. In the last year, every push against the German army had ground to a halt in the wet mud almost before it had begun. The British army had suffered terrible losses for little benefit and the morale of the troops was the lowest it had ever been. All through the trenches the men were resigned to their lot - at best they were tired, wet and hungry; at worst they were frightened of what horrors each day would bring. When an offensive was imminent, as now, every man would become pre-occupied with his own thoughts and fears and although it was rare for a man to crack up in such circumstances, Nathan had heard of it happening. There were rumours only the week before that an officer had been forced, in self defence, to shoot a man who had gone berserk. Cowardice in the face of the enemy was a military crime of the highest degree, punishable by the firing squad - it was far better to take your chances, slim as they might be, in front of the German machine guns.

Nathan ordered a flare to be fired and in its sudden harsh glare took a glance through the periscope. The view caused his stomach to churn. In the next twenty four hours he would have to face the desolate landscape in front of him twice. There was nothing but mud, shell craters, barbed wire and more mud. Any trees had long since disappeared. He was sure that in later life, should he survive, he would be haunted by the mud and the rain. He could see the German lines clearly, as they could the British, he thought sourly, and as always nothing was showing apart from the sandbagged parapets.

A night patrol in no man's land was dreaded by everyone. You were completely exposed if a flare went up from the other side, or worse still from your own side, and were a sitting target for any reasonably able sniper. Nathan shuddered and having noted the sections of wire he needed to cut, turned away as the scene plunged into darkness again. Minutes later, under the cover of the darkness, which now seemed inadequate, he and his two volunteers hauled themselves over the parapet of the trench and slid into the mud, flattening themselves to the ground immediately. Motionless for what seemed like an eternity, they waited. Then, cautiously, Nathan raised his head and motioned to the two men to move forward. All three began a snake like slither through the mud away from the comparative safety of their own trenches, towards the barbed wire and the enemy.

Sliding his way through the slimy mud, Nathan's heightened senses were almost overwhelmed with fear. He was sure his companions felt the same. At any moment an enemy flare could go up and the three of them would be facing death. But nothing happened. They reached the first barrier of barbed wire without event and went quietly to work, snipping away at the sharp barbs with wire-cutters. The wire was never ending and the minutes were like hours to each of the three men; Nathan was particularly conscious of the passing time; every minute they spent away from the trench increased their chances of being discovered.

After some time of cutting, Nathan signaled a pause and began to wonder just how much wire Urquahart expected him to cut, even though he knew the answer would be as much as possible. Time was running out and he motioned to the other two to resume cutting while he took a good look at the German lines. Everything seemed still, but he had the unmistakable feeling that someone was watching him.

No sooner had this thought entered his mind than it turned into reality as a flare went off above them. Nathan flattened himself to the ground, one of the others following suit without prompting. The other man, a private who Nathan knew had been a fisherman, but whose name he could not remember, had, to Nathan's horror, frozen with fear. Before Nathan could do anything, he bolted. He'd not made more than five yards before machine gun fire almost cut him in half and he fell to the ground without even the time to scream.

"Oh dear Christ in Heaven" whispered the other private, fear almost depriving him of his voice.

"Don't move!" hissed Nathan, speaking through a mouthful of mud, knowing as he spoke that the last thing the other man was going to do was move. Silently, Nathan began to pray, knowing that any second the deadly hail of bullets would come their way. But it did not. The landscape once more fell into darkness and silence. Nathan lay still for a long time, but still nothing happened. Finally, too tense to remain still any longer, he whispered "We've got to get back to our own trench. I'll go first, you follow but stay on your belly!". Nathan began the long slither back towards his own lines, still expecting a hail of death at any moment. The silence began to prey on his mind and he imagined he could hear rifle bolts being drawn back and then a flare went up and a machine gun started. To his surprise he found himself near a shell crater and he launched himself into it, but not before agonising pain in his leg brought a scream from his lips. He collapsed into his hole and gratefully sank into oblivion.

The cold woke him after only a few minutes. Lying in the water at the bottom of the shell hole, his leg agony and bleeding profusely, Nathan knew the next few hours would decide his future, would determine whether he would live or die. He had no idea what had become of the other private. Grimly, he thought to himself that this was it. There was nowhere to run. And that thought brought a sombre smile to his lips. Even if there was a way out, with his leg injured, and he didn't know how badly, would he be able to move anyway?

The sky lit up again. Nathan wasn't sure if it was a flare or a shell, as his hearing seemed to be gone. He noticed a greenish cloud drifting towards him and the British lines before he slipped back into unconsciousness.

He woke suddenly to find himself screaming and gasping for breath sprawled across the otherwise empty bed at Smallbrook, sheets in disarray. He was shaking and sweat was pouring off him. Dry-mouthed and thirsty, and with feelings of despair and terror, he climbed out of bed and pulled some clothes on. There was no water in the bedroom, he would have to go to the kitchen for that, but the tablets Doctor Allerby had given him were in his kit-bag in the cupboard. He'd thankfully not needed them since coming to Smallbrook, having only had the dream occasionally between returning to Dalton Combe and moving out to the farm. He took the two tablets with a hastily gulped glass of water in the kitchen, having almost fallen down the steep stairs, and sat at the table, drained and lonely, waiting for the shaking to stop.

Chapter Twenty-three

The journey to Smallbrook from Hereford had been awful, for both Jenny and Edward. The first part had been the easiest, as Doctor Dougall had arranged for them to be taken across the city to the station by a Red Cross ambulance. Negotiating the station itself was also easy, as staff were used to dealing with wounded soldiers, and it was the same friendly helpful porter that had met Jenny when she first arrived.

"Leaving us to be off home, are you?" he said, recognising her. "And taking your man with you I see." Jenny nodded, smiling, but before she could speak, the man carried on, speaking this time to Edward. "A man needs a good woman to look after him, don't you agree, sir?" Much to Jenny's embarrassment, Edward did nothing but grunt in reply. "Never mind," said the guard, addressing Jenny once more," I'm sure he'll have a smile on his face after he's been home a few days." Edward was already beginning to show signs of irritation after being transferred from the ambulance to his wheelchair, which was a bulky cumbersome affair. He'd immediately started to complain that it was uncomfortable.

For Jenny, the journey south was even more arduous and uncomfortable than her earlier trip in the other direction had been. With Edward in his wheelchair, the only place they could travel on the train was in the guards van, something else which fuelled Edward's annoyance.

"I feel like a piece of bloody luggage," had been his comment. The elderly guard, a cheerful man, had tried his best to lighten the mood, but to no avail. Finally he left them to themselves and shut himself in his own little room at the back of the van.

Much to Jenny's anguish, things got worse at Dalton Magna, the nearest railway stop to Dalton Combe. Changing trains at Bristol and Exeter had gone smoothly, despite Edward's moaning, but for some reason, at Dalton Magna, presumably to do with it being a small rural halt rather than an station, the platform was some inches below the level of the door of the guards van. This wasn't a problem for the passenger coaches, with their external steps, but was proving quite an obstacle for Edward in his wheelchair.

With the guard scratching his head and wondering how he would get Edward and the chair safely down onto the platform, Jenny was pleased to see Nathan waiting there, and waved out to him. He waved back, smiling.

"Who's that?" Edward snarled in an undertone that the guard couldn't hear.

"That's Nathan, Eddie. He's the one I told you about who's been helping me at Smallbrook." Edward took a long hard look and saw a handsome dark haired man of medium height standing on the platform, and said nothing. It wasn't what he'd expected. He had been expecting an older man when Jenny had told him he'd been a sergeant.

"Pleased to meet you, Mr Tiley," Nathan said in welcome, not knowing whether or not to extend his hand for a handshake.

"Holt," said Edward inclining his head slightly towards him

as you would to a servant, Nathan thought irritably, or perhaps a junior rank in the army. Between them, with the use of a ramp the guard had remembered he had, he and Nathan soon had Edward safely onto the platform. Thanking the guard, Jenny then began to wheel him away.

Following behind with Edward's trunk on a trolley, Nathan could not hear the words that were being spoken between Edward and Jenny, but he knew that Edward was complaining about something as she pushed his chair along the platform towards the exit. He had the feeling there were difficult times ahead at Smallbrook Farm and not just for him, but for everyone. Edward Tiley did not seem to be a very approachable man.

Even with such a small station there was a waiting room, thankfully empty and Jenny wheeled the still talking Edward straight through and out into the lane, to a waiting wagon, which Edward looked at with some distaste but luckily without comment. George Wilkins came around from the horse in a cloud of pipe smoke.

"Good day to you, Mr Tiley. Nice to see you again," he said, politely removing the pipe from his mouth as he spoke, and noticing Edward's look regarding the wagon. "Your carriage awaits," he added with a mischievous smile, gesturing towards the old vehicle with his pipe. Edward, who had been on the verge of berating Jenny about the wagon, smiled and held out his hand to awkwardly shake the old farmer's own outstretched hand. George Wilkins was someone Edward has always looked up to, not just because he was their landlord but also because he was the closest thing Dalton Combe had to gentry.

"It feels good to be back, Mr Wilkins," Edward replied, and Nathan noticed, possibly with a slightly jaundiced eye, he was suddenly all smiles and charm. He was already beginning to dislike Jenny's returning husband.

It was a struggle to get the wheelchair and its occupant into the back of the wagon. George Wilkins, having foreseen the difficulty of the wagon bed being so far above the ground, had brought two solid-looking planks with him, but Nathan and George Wilkins still had a great deal of pushing and heaving, along with a wobble or two, before they finally managed to secure the chair firmly. Jenny climbed in beside Edward, and then sat on his trunk. Nathan joined the old farmer on the seat in front of the couple.

The ensuing journey back to Smallbrook was not as comfortable as any of them would have liked it to be, but in the presence of George Wilkins, Nathan noticed that Edward kept his complaints, if not to himself, then at least for Jenny's ears only. The wagon, despite George Wilkins' best efforts, jerked, jolted and juddered all the way to Dalton Combe in the ruts of the dry lanes, while Nathan lost himself in his thoughts, not in the mood for conversation.

One of his concerns, perhaps his main concern, was still whether or not to stay at Smallbrook, a concern heightened by actually having met Edward. The man was plainly going to be difficult to get along with. And while Jenny would undoubtedly need his help with the farm work, and possibly with Edward himself, Nathan couldn't see Edward Tiley being happy with the situation. He was also finding it very hard to see past the end of his happy relationship with Jenny.

She was in his thoughts every second he was awake. There had been other women, but none whom he had felt much attachment to, and while he'd certainly hoped he would fall in love someday and meet someone to spend the rest of his life with, he'd thought it would be something gradual, a growing respect developing into a spark that became a flame as they came to know each other. He had not envisaged falling in love to be quite so dramatic. Now Edward was back in her life, Nathan was at a loss as to what to do, or even what to think. Confident that Jenny felt the same way for him as he did for her, Nathan could see no possible way of the three of them handling the situation. As things stood now, he thought miserably, Edward was in law and before God her husband, and he, Nathan, nothing more than an adulterer.

"Nathan!" Jenny's voice was quite sharp and jerked him out of his reverie. It was the third time she'd called him, but he'd been so deep in thought he'd not heard. She actually thought he might have gone to sleep, despite the awkward motion of the wagon. He turned in his seat to see her face looking up at him. Edward was gazing back down the lane along which they had travelled, paying no attention to them. "Is everything ready for Edward at Smallbrook?" she asked.

"Yes," he replied, "I've done everything I thought would be needed for him." Her smile was all the thanks he wanted, better than any words. He turned once more to face the road, but not before he had seen Edward's back and shoulders stiffen as if in anger.

"It's going to be a rough time ahead, lad," George Wilkins said quietly, speaking softly so only Nathan would hear his words. "And it's in my mind that young Mrs Tiley is going to need more help than ever at Smallbrook." Nathan nodded, and although the older man was concentrating on the road and the horse and didn't appear to notice, he must have sensed Nathan's agreement. For the rest of the journey, both they and Edward and Jenny remained quiet, but it was an uneasy quiet, not a comfortable silence.

The wagon provoked no interest in Dalton Combe as they passed through, but it seemed to Jenny that Edward hunkered down as they approached the first cottages. She put her hand on his arm, but he pulled away without even looking at her. It was not until after the wagon had carefully negotiated the narrow bridge at the bottom end of the village, that bridge only just wide enough to take a wagon this size that Edward seemed to recover his composure. It was just ten minutes later that George Wilkins manoeuvred his wagon into the farmyard at Smallbrook. Edward's luggage was quickly taken into the house, followed fairly quickly by Edward, who was easily wheeled down by George and Nathan. Jenny then wheeled him rather bumpily into the farm kitchen, the two men following.

Nathan was quite pleased with the changes he'd made in the kitchen to accommodate Edward since hearing from Jenny that he was returning to Smallbrook with her. The bed he'd moved downstairs was so placed, if the curtain was pulled back, as to allow Edward to be able to see everything going on the kitchen, and also to allow him a good view of the farmyard through the open farmhouse door. The risk of any curious chickens wandering into the house was one that would have to be endured. A cabinet had been placed next to the bed for a lamp and a small sideboard had been emptied to take Edward's clothes. The curtain, when pulled across, would give him some privacy. Jenny was delighted with the arrangements, but her smile was not to last long. Edward most definitely was not happy and glared at her.

"Is this it? Is this all the privacy I get? To spend my days and nights in a kitchen?"

"We thought it would be the best place, Eddie," Jenny began.

"We? You didn't ask me!"

"I meant that Nathan and I..."

"Nathan! First name terms with the help? What right has he to be making decisions that affect me?" Edward's voice had risen to the point where he was shouting, forgetting George Wilkins' presence in his anger. Nathan spoke before an obviously upset Jenny could reply to her husband.

"What is it that you want, then Mr Tiley? To be left all alone all day upstairs in one of the bedrooms like some invalid aunt? Or to be involved in the farm down here, where you can see what's going on?" Nathan was barely controlling his anger. He felt George Wilkins' hand on his arm as Edward turned his anger in his direction.

"It's Lieutenant Tiley to you, Holt, and it has nothing to do with you anyway! This is between me and my wife." He emphasised the final two words.

"We're not in the bloody army now," Nathan said sharply, "and Mr Tiley will suit me just fine." Jenny was beginning to look more and more upset and George Wilkins increased the pressure on Nathan's arm, pulling him back towards the door.

"Come on, lad. Let's get outside," he said. He closed the door behind them but they could still hear the raised voices as the reunited husband and wife argued. "Nathan, lad, mark my words, there's going to be hard times ahead for that young woman." Nathan said nothing, his temper cooling slowly. "She's going to need help here."

"What can I do? I can't stay here. It wouldn't be right – they're man and wife" Nathan said quietly. "And you've seen what he's like." The raised voices continued in the kitchen.

"She needs you, lad. Think on that. Would you really leave her alone with him?" George turned away. "I have to get back to Manor Farm," he continued. "Think on what I've said, but tread careful."

Chapter Twenty-four

Edward Tiley was finding it much more difficult than he'd expected to accept his life at Smallbrook. He was totally dependent on Jenny and on Holt, which not only greatly annoyed him, it also deeply embarrassed him. It had somehow been different in the hospital, more impersonal, more clinical, just easier to deal with. To have to call his wife, or worse still, that man Holt, who he was convinced was sleeping with his wife, was nothing less than humiliating. He couldn't move from this bed without the man's help. And that wheelchair contraption. It had seemed a good idea, but he'd started disliking it on the train journey from Hereford. For a few days after arriving at the farm he'd refused to use it. After an argument with Jenny, yet another in what seemed to be a constant flow, he'd agreed to being wheeled around the farm, inevitably almost becoming a cropper on rough ground. That was two weeks before and he'd not been in it since.

Today however was going to be different. Jenny had offered to take him out to the orchard, which was to become the centre of activity at the farm because the cider-maker was due. He'd agreed, although slightly reluctantly, but now the day had come around, he was quite looking forward to getting out. The visit of the travelling cider-press was always a high point of the year for him and an event for the local farmers Even Manor Farm, big as it was, was unable to support its own cider making equipment and relied on the travelling press. A light tapping on the door interrupted his thoughts just as he was about to doze off.

"Come in," he called. The door opened and a wizened, worn looking man in a battered cap and equally battered jacket appeared. Edward noticed that his trousers were held up with braces and baling twine instead of a belt. The visitor quickly whipped off his cap, revealing a mess of white hair, but Edward was still unable to gauge the age of the man, who looked surprised at seeing the bed in the kitchen. Edward saw, or thought he saw pity or horror or both when the stranger noticed the scarring on his face and then the absence of feet and lower legs in the shape under the blankets. "What do you want?" he said to him, scowling.

"I...I was lookin' for Mrs Tiley," the man said, and then paused, looking more closely at Edward than Edward liked. "It's Mr Tiley, isn't it? What went off to France with the Yeomanry?" Edward nodded, irritably uncomfortable under the man's gaze. "But I 'eard you was dead, sir."

"No," replied Edward, "But maybe I should be," he added bitterly. "You'll find my wife somewhere around the farmyard, probably with that man Holt." Thanking him the old man turned towards the door, but was surprised to see Edward lift his left hand, which had been hanging by the side of the bed, and awkwardly place a revolver on the bedside table. He said nothing, but closed the door firmly behind him. He found Nathan before he found Jenny, and Nathan noticed the old man looking a little pale.

"Is there something wrong?" he asked.

"Wrong?" the man exclaimed. "He's got a gun in there, you know."

"A gun? What do you mean?" As far as Nathan was aware there wasn't even a shotgun at Smallbrook.

"Mr Tiley was holding a pistol by the side of the bed. I was only asking after Mrs Tiley."

"You'll find her over by the milking shed. Is it about the cider?" The man nodded and Nathan added "I'll be back out to help in a few minutes." After a short pause, with his hand on the man's shoulder, Nathan continued. "Don't say anything about this, will you?" The man nodded and before entering the kitchen, Nathan watched him cross the farmyard to look for Jenny.

"What do you want, Holt?" Edward demanded. "Haven't you got work to do?"

"Where's the gun?" Nathan asked, ignoring the barbed insult and crossing to the bed, where he stood over Edward looking down at him. Edward turned his head, deliberately avoiding Nathan's gaze. "Where's the gun, Tiley?"

"In the bedside cabinet." There seemed little point in denying he had one.

"Have you got ammunition?"

"What's the point of a gun without bullets, Holt?" Edward snapped. "Of course I've got ammunition."

"Why do you need a gun here at Smallbrook?"

"A man never knows when he's got to protect what's his,"

181

Edward said meaningfully. "Someone might want to take it away from you. Anyway, it's none of your business."

"Does Jenny know?"

"What kind of man keeps secrets from his wife? Or a wife from her husband, for that matter."

"Does she know you've got a gun?"Nathan repeated, a coldness entering his voice.

"No."

"Let's keep it that way shall we?" said Nathan in a tone that brooked no argument. With every intention of removing the weapon as soon as he had the opportunity, Nathan turned his back on Edward, and stormed out into the farmyard. He caught up with Jenny and the cider-man at the gate to the orchard. Jenny introduced the man to Nathan as Archie Sansome, and two other men who had arrived with him were moving the press into the orchard. Offers of a cup of tea before starting were politely declined, mainly because Archie had little desire to return to the kitchen with its gun-wielding invalid. Jenny then went back to see Edward.

As soon as she saw him and recognised his mood, she was glad that she could manage the task of getting him out of bed and into the wheelchair on her own. He looked furious and she wondered what had sparked off this particular mood. She fixed a smile on her face.

"They're just getting ready in the orchard," she said.

"Time to wheel out the cripple, then, is it?" he replied.

"Oh don't be like that, Edward. It's a lovely day out there and you know the doctor said it would do you good to be outside." All she received in return was a scowl and a grunt. He did however allow Jenny to help him off the bed and into the chair without further complaint. She carefully tucked a blanket over the lower part of his body ignoring the fact that it just dangled down where his legs should have been. It took her a few minutes to manoeuvre the cumbersome machine out of the house, but they were soon in the orchard, where preparations for the day's work were almost complete.

Jenny pushed the chair into a shady spot after Archie had warily introduced his workmen to Edward, and left him alone while she joined the others. At first still feeling angry and then frustrated about not being able to help with the activities, Edward soon found himself interested in what was going on. He'd missed the last two autumn apple harvests at Smallbrook. For the first he'd been training with the County Militia prior to being sent to France, and the second he'd spent close to death, unconscious and almost comatose in a grimy field hospital. Not that he remembered much about that, thankfully. At neither time had he thought about Smallbrook or indeed his wife. At that time, his had been a violent world far removed from cider-making.

With the pulping machine starting only reluctantly, most of the early activity was under the trees, where Jenny and Nathan were gathering the piled fruit into canvas buckets and carrying them to the pulper where they were passed to Archie and one of his assistants and the contents tipped into the hopper.

The other man, who'd been introduced by Archie as

Hezekiah, but who insisted on being called Hez as he preferred it to what he termed his 'Sunday name,' was busy preparing the press for the first load of apple pulp which would shortly be produced by the pulper.

On each of his trips to the pulper with baskets of fruit, Nathan was extremely conscious of Edward watching him, and the man was having the effect of a dark cloud on an otherwise beautiful sunny day. Nathan couldn't shake off the thought of the gun that Edward had hidden. How did he still have a service weapon, and what on earth made him think he needed it here on this peaceful farm? It was going to be a worry, especially considering the frame of mind in which Edward Tiley spent his days.

"Holt!" Edward's voice somehow cut across the noise of the pulping machine like a barked parade ground command. Nathan passed his bucket up to Archie and turned to face Edward, who was beckoning him across to where he sat in his wheelchair. Edward was obviously uncomfortable and a little angry, and with a burst of sympathy, Nathan felt he could understand why. Edward was a proud man, and it must come hard to have to publicly ask for help from anybody. The thought didn't stop Nathan from disliking the man. Archie had looked up at the sharpness in Edward's tone, but Nathan just smiled and winked at him. Archie went back to his work. As Nathan reached him, Edward said "I've had enough of this. I need to get back to the house."

"Do you need Jenny as well?" Nathan asked. Edward nodded in response, not looking at Nathan. Although Jenny needed Nathan's help to get Edward back into his bed, they had decided, without consulting Edward, that it would be Jenny alone who helped with any personal needs. Nathan crossed to Jenny and then told Archie to take a ten minute break. Before Nathan and Jenny had even left the orchard with Edward, the three old men were happily filling their pipes.

By the time Nathan was back in the orchard, leaving Jenny with her husband, the men were back at work. The pulp from the machine was wrapped in cloth often traditionally made from horse-hair, which was what Hez preferred, and placed in trays which were then stacked on the press in what was called a 'cheese'. The juice extracted from the apple pulp by the squeezing action of the press was run off into the odd collection of casks which Nathan had brought round to the orchard from the barn. It would be left to ferment for up to six weeks before the casks were sealed and the contents allowed to mature. Nothing was left to waste, and Nathan found himself messily gathering up the remaining apple pulp from the press to be used as feed for the farm animals during the winter. He was just preparing to return to gathering buckets of fruit when he noticed Jenny coming back to the orchard. It was plain that she'd been crying.

Chapter Twenty-five

It was an argument with Edward of course. The rows and bad feeling had been increasing recently and disturbing the peace and equilibrium of life at Smallbrook. Nathan, although not liking it, was slowly becoming accustomed to seeing Jenny upset, but this was the first time since Edward's return that he had seen her reduced to tears by him. He wouldn't have the opportunity to find out what it was about until the end of the day. As work continued in the orchard Jenny remained subdued and her mood was nowhere near as happy as it had been first thing in the morning. She prepared and provided lunch for them all under the trees, eating her own in the kitchen with Edward and it was not until late in the afternoon that Nathan saw the beginnings of a smile on her face on hearing that the work was going to be finished that day. She was almost back to her normal self by the time she left the orchard to milk her cows.

Archie and his men were sleeping in the barn overnight before moving on the following morning. It wasn't until the three men had shared an evening meal made slightly uncomfortable by Edward insisting on eating on his own behind his curtain, and retired to the barn to literally 'hit the hay' that Nathan and Jenny found themselves able to talk. Even so, it was in whispers as they were conscious of Edward's presence.

"Something's been upsetting you all day, Jenny," Nathan said. He inclined his head towards Edward's end of the room, a look of query on his face. She nodded.

"It's not easy," she said so quietly that Nathan had to strain to catch her words. It was likely that Edward was asleep, but it was safer not to take any chances. "He doesn't really mean it, Nathan. He never used to be like this." Nathan was already sure of that, sure that Jenny would not have married Edward in the first place if he had been. He smiled at her affectionately as she went on. "It must all have been so terrible for him." Nathan thought of his own dreams and what he himself had been through and found himself agreeing with Jenny. What Edward had suffered was more than enough to turn any man's mind.

"But that doesn't give him the right to take it out on other people, especially you. He's turning on the people trying to help him." He paused. "So what was it all about today?" Jenny didn't answer him at first, then sighed.

"Everything. He's a very unhappy man, Nathan." He just looked at her, at how tired and sad she looked, thinking to himself that Edward was doing a very good job of making her just as unhappy. The thought must have been apparent on his face and she took his hand, giving it a gentle squeeze. "Don't worry about me, Nathan, please. I'm alright. Eddie can't help it and I understand that." She wasn't to be drawn any more on the subject. They chatted for a while, talking about safe matters concerning the farm and then Nathan wished her goodnight and walked across to the barn to climb to his bed in the hayloft. Once more he found himself unable to sleep, worrying about what he could possibly do to help Jenny and to stop her husband was making her life a misery.

Edward was also unable to sleep. He'd heard Jenny and Nathan's whispered conversation without actually being able to make out the words and it annoyed him, adding to his suspicions about them both. Every word, every look and above all every smile was extra fuel for the fire of jealousy sparked the first time he'd seen Nathan. The same fire that flickered whenever they were both out and about and working around the farm and he could only worry and fret about what they might be doing. But he was going to bide his time until they made a mistake and he knew for certain.

Sleep was so long in coming for Edward that when he woke the next morning he was more tetchy than usual. A quiet, almost silent breakfast was followed by the usual enquiry from Jenny about whether he wanted to sit outside in the sunshine or not, an offer he dismissed curtly, earning a sharp look from Nathan which he ignored. After yesterday in the orchard, he was most certainly not going to sit outside the farmhouse door in the sunshine, wrapped up like an old man and watching the chickens scratching around in the dirt. Nathan and Jenny left him to his mood which began to spiral ever downwards.

The farmhouse door was open and a slight refreshing breeze was blowing through the kitchen. It also gave Edward the chance to see what was going on outside in the farmyard if he wanted to, with a further view to the fields beyond. Fields he would never walk in again, he thought to himself irritably. But it was the creaking of the door leading to the stairs from the kitchen that was holding Edward's attention. It had not been fastened properly and as it moved, barely an inch, in the light gusts of air, the pained creaking of the old hinges was like torture. Lying in his bed, there was nothing Edward could do about it.

His irritation at the incessant creaking was just one symptom of his ever-worsening mood, with one negative thought leading to another. Coming to Smallbrook from the Infirmary had been what he had wanted, but he wasn't happy. He found he hated Smallbrook Farm just as much as he had hated the hospital. No, he didn't hate Smallbrook, he thought. He hated being helpless; he couldn't appreciate Smallbrook. He couldn't get out there to have the chance to appreciate it. Idly, his fingers caressed the revolver he now had hidden under his blankets. He knew Holt intended to take it from him and he wasn't prepared to let that happen.

Soon he was listing and reviewing one depressing thought after another in his mind. The list of things he would never do again was endless. And that damned door was creaking exactly in time with pounding headache he was beginning to develop. Jenny came into sight outside, walking across the farmyard, and waved at him. That simple action brought him up sharply, for his biggest regret, and the loss that made the fire of his anger burn most brightly was that he would never again be able to hold Jenny, never feel the warmth of her body, never make love with her again the way they had used to. The anger suddenly felt like an explosion waiting to happen.

Hearing Nathan's voice outside calling to Jenny was almost too much for him, certain as he was that the man was certainly doing with Jenny what he was unable to as her husband. His fingers tightened around the gun. For God's sake, he thought, I can't even deal with a creaking door by myself. He finally erupted.

"Holt! Damn you Holt, get in here!" he shouted impatiently. Then, as Nathan entered the kitchen, added "Where the bloody hell have you been, Holt. You took your time."

"Did you want something?" Nathan was in no mood to be polite, but still tried hard to ignore Edward's rudeness. One of the cows had kicked his injured leg, whilst being milked. Nathan had jumped in pain and watched in despair as a whole bucket of milk slopped over the cowshed floor.

"Of course I want something! Do you think I'd waste my time shouting for you if I didn't? Do something about that damned door creaking!" he said pointing at the door to the stairs. It was an order, barked at Nathan, who trying to take into account, once more, the suffering of the other man, sighed deeply and did as he was instructed, but without saying a word.

"In the army, Holt, I'd have you on a charge for dumb insolence," Edward continued, his voice a little lower. Nathan looked over his shoulder while fastening the wayward door.

"But we're not in the Army, are we?" he said calmly. "And I would have thought an officer and a gentleman like yourself would have better manners anyway."

"Is this the hired help telling me to be polite?" Edward asked sharply, angered even more by Nathan's calm reply.

"I'm no hired help, as you well know, and yes, I am. Good manners cost nothing, no matter who you're speaking to."

"Not the hired help eh? Then what are you doing here, man?" Nathan's attitude was not what Edward expected or wanted. "Do you think I'm stupid, that I don't know what's going on?" Nathan eyed him coldly, not responding. "Nothing to say, Holt? Don't you want to tell me how you get your payment in other ways? Is she good, Holt? Is she worth it?" Nathan stepped across to the bed-ridden man, leaning over him fists clenched, his face thunderous. Edward looked up at him, not in the least bit intimidated, just further angered.

"I want you out of this house and off this farm, Holt!"

"I'll certainly get out of the house, but as for the farm, it's got nothing to do with you. My arrangement is with Jenny. If she tells me to go, I'll go."

"I'm sure your 'arrangement' is very satisfactory, Holt." Edward's fingers stroked the barrel of the revolver as he spoke. "But you listen, it's my bloody farm, and I want you out of here, now!"

"Edward! Nathan! Stop it! Both of you!" Jenny, having coming into the kitchen unknown to either of them, placed herself firmly between the two angry men. "Edward, Nathan helps here because we need him to. You know that. I couldn't run this place on my own."

"Oh yes, let's not forget you're married to a cripple who can't do a thing! Holt helps here for what he gets from you!" Edward was beside himself with anger, his fingers tight around the gun's butt. "I'm no fool, woman. But sharing his bed to get work done around the farm? I'd never have believed it of you." Edward looked disgustedly at his wife. "And if you're doing that, just what does that make you, eh?" Jenny looked at him aghast. "Stuck for words? Whore is the one you're looking for!" he shouted. Nathan was as astonished as Edward when Jenny swung her open hand back and slapped him hard across the face before rushing upstairs from the kitchen, crying. Withdrawing his hand from under the blankets, Edward rubbed the now sore spot on his face.

"You bastard, Tiley," Nathan growled. "Can't you see how much she cares for you, and how much you're pushing her away?" Unsure if he would be able to control his own anger, Nathan stormed out into the farmyard, leaving Edward by himself.

Harsh words once spoken stay spoken and serve to keep already inflamed tempers fiercely alight. Nathan avoided Edward completely, allowing the man's words to take a firm hold in his mind, while Jenny, needing to be in and out of the kitchen, simply ignored Edward, not speaking when placing a meal in front of him or when seeing to his needs. Nathan ate his lunchtime meal in the barn. There was a tangible atmosphere around the farm which all three of them seemed to be aware of, but could do nothing about. Inevitably, arguments broke out again in the afternoon.

Nathan, walking across the farmyard after carrying some repairs to Smallbrook's ramshackle hen-house, heard raised voices in the farmhouse kitchen once more. He put his tools away in the barn and when he crossed back towards the house, they were still raised. He paused by the kitchen door, not liking to eavesdrop, but not wishing to go in and become entangled in another row, particularly one between husband and wife. He didn't like what he heard from inside or the effect it might have on

Jenny.

"For God's sake, Jenny stop arguing with me! My mind's made up. We're leaving the farm," Nathan heard Edward shout at Jenny.

"But you can't," he heard her reply quietly. She sounded close to tears.

"Why not? Old Wilkins can have the place back and good riddance." Edward seemed to have no other tone of voice but shouting.

"But what are you going to do then? Where will you live? Who will look after you?" she asked, the questions following each other rapidly. Nathan found himself unable to do anything but carry on listening. Edward seemed even angrier than usual.

"You'll look after me. We're leaving and you'll do as you're told, Jenny," Nathan heard him shout.

"No, I won't. This is my home and this is not going to happen!" To Nathan she sounded almost frustrated with anger. "You're not going to take my home away from me!" There was a strong edge of stubbornness in her voice. Nathan shook his head and moved away from the doorway. He was not by nature an eavesdropper and certainly didn't want to hear any more of this particular argument. He had just reached the far side of the farmyard when he heard the farmhouse door bang against the frame. It was Jenny, and he could hear her crying from where he was as she turned her face to the wall by the door. Edward was still shouting and cursing, his words indistinct to Nathan until he re-crossed the farmyard to be with Jenny. Then he clearly heard

194

Edward's last comments as he reached her and put his arm around her shoulder.

"You scheming bitch! It's my bloody farm, not yours!" Something hit the wall inside and smashed.

"Is everything all right?" he asked. She nodded, without looking at him.

"He wants us to leave Smallbrook," she said, turning her head to look at him. Her face was tear-streaked and flushed.

"I thought it was just me he wanted to go," said Nathan, attempting a half-smile. "What did you say to make so angry?"

"He says it's no place for him to live, and that I can't look after him properly here," Jenny said, "and then I told him it's not his farm anyway."

"He should have thought about being looked after before insisting you bring him back here," Nathan said. "But what do you mean it's not his farm?" He stroked a strand of hair away from her face and was surprised when she almost flinched at his touch.

"George Wilkins signed over the tenancy to me when we heard of Edward's death. The farm's in my name, not his." Despite the seriousness of the situation, Nathan felt an urge to laugh, then Jenny impulsively threw her arms around him and hugged him tight, kissing him passionately. He could feel the tears on her cheeks and the tension in her body.

Nathan, surprised at the embrace, felt the sudden flash of his anger at Edward begin to slip away. His arms went around her, a warm feeling enveloping him, a mixture of passion and affection, just the sheer joy of holding her close. He pulled her closer, neither of them noticing that the farmhouse door, although slammed, had not latched and had swung slightly open.

Inside the kitchen, Edward's anger and frustration had reached boiling point. With the door slightly open, Edward could see Nathan and Jenny, as after all they had sited his bed to give him a good view of the farmyard, and he saw their passionate embrace. It was all he needed to confirm his suspicions about their relationship and all of a sudden he felt very tired, very alone and very, very angry while the gun under his hand in the bed felt very good indeed.

Chapter Twenty-six

Enough was enough as far as Nathan was concerned. The situation at Smallbrook had deteriorated so quickly and badly over the last few days that both he and Jenny had decided they needed some help. The arguments of the day before had been the final straw. Smallbrook was not the place for Edward Tiley. It was not what he needed, and Jenny suspected, not what he wanted now he was there. Unknown to her, Edward had reached the same decision during the night. His feeling of triumph at having his suspicions about Jenny and Nathan vindicated had rapidly descended into a storm of despondency, leaving him or so he felt, with few options. He was too proud a man to let the situation go on much longer.

Nathan just wanted what was best for Jenny, suggesting that they turn to Reverend Simpkins for advice, and he now paused for a few moments at the rectory gate to gather his thoughts and to a certain extent, his courage. People in the village had begun to talk and gossip since Edward's return to Smallbrook and although Nathan knew that Reverend Simpkins was a pleasant enough man, very approachable and easy to talk to, the moral and spiritual life of the village was effectively in his hands. He simply didn't know the vicar's opinion of the current situation

Nathan had never been to the rectory before and had never actually properly seen the building, screened as it was from the village by a line of overgrown leilandi. He was surprised by the building as he walked down the short drive which sloped towards the house and the river slightly beyond it. The house looked almost neglected, which he supposed was hardly a surprise as he knew from Joshua and Martha, but mostly Martha, that the vicar lived in only three rooms of the large sixteen room building. Designed for a large Victorian family, it was simply too big to look after for a single man and the Reverend Simpkins' concerns lay more with the spiritual welfare of his flock than with the material welfare of his own dwelling.

It was a smiling Reverend Simpkins, rather than his housekeeper, who answered the door when Nathan rang the bell-pull.

"Ah, Nathan. Hello. Would it surprise you if I said I'd been expecting you?"

"No, not really," replied Nathan, smiling in return. The vicar nodded.

"Won't you come in? I'll have Mrs Nesbitt make us some tea." Nathan was ushered through to a light airy sitting room that obviously doubled as the vicar's study, with untidy piles of books and manuscripts everywhere. Reverend Simpkins, moving some papers off a chair, gestured for Nathan to sit down, and after arranging with Mrs Nesbitt, who came in to the Rectory to clean and cook for him, to organise some tea, sat down himself behind a cluttered desk.

"Although I've been thinking you might call, it would be wrong of me to assume that I know why you're here, so how can I help you Nathan?" the older man asked.

"I would guess that you do know why I'm here, vicar,"

smiled Nathan. "I've come to ask for help for Jenny."

"And what sort of help do you or Jenny think I can offer?" the vicar asked. He'd remembered Jenny's preference for the use of her first name. Nathan explained about Edward's moods and anger and how it was affecting Jenny, while the vicar listened sympathetically. Talks with Dr Allerby had alerted him to a problem at Smallbrook and his ears were ever open for talk around the village. Mrs Nesbitt never let him down in that area. The village as a whole was quietly aware that things were amiss at Smallbrook Farm and Reverend Simpkins knew he could do no less than help in any way he felt able.

"We ... she ... I ... well, we were hoping you could talk to him, or get him to talk to you," Nathan said.

"I remember Edward Tiley, Nathan. A down-to-earth, generally straight-speaking sort of man. It's a delicate situation. Is he looking for some one to open his soul to? Does he want to confess his sins?" the vicar asked, a twinkle in his eye. "Or does he want to complain about someone else's?" Nathan felt uncomfortable under the vicar's gaze.

"No, nothing like that. He is a bitter man, vicar, angry with everything and everyone, including himself."

"For someone who has suffered so much, that is sadly not such a surprise. A very great pity, but not a surprise. Would he agree to see me?"

"I honestly don't know. But he needs help, vicar. Jenny needs help."

"I'll come tomorrow." Reverend Simpkins' decision

199

surprised Nathan and he began to offer his thanks. "No need. I can't turn my back on anyone who needs help. Now, what's happened to that tea?"

Although chatty during their refreshments, Reverend Simpkins had seemed a little distant and it was as Nathan was rising to leave that the vicar surprised him again. The older man also rose from his chair, presumably to see him to the door, Nathan thought. But instead, the vicar walked past him and opened the study door to let himself out.

"Can you wait here a moment while I get my hat and coat?" he said, and walked off. When he returned and noticed the look on Nathan's face, he smiled. "I've decided to walk back with you now. It will give us both some company along the lane to Smallbrook Farm, and I think the matter of Edward Tiley needs addressing with some urgency, don't you?" He smiled again, not needing or waiting for an answer. "Well, come along then."

For an older man, Reverend Simpkins set a good pace, and Nathan, with his leg hindering him, at first struggled to keep up. Noticing, the vicar apologised, slowing down to a more comfortable pace for his companion.

"There's no need to apologise, vicar. I'm just not as quick as I used to be, but there are many far worse off than me, including Edward Tiley." The vicar nodded, and then appeared to be deep in thought for a few moments.

"I've seen some lads in Exeter," he began, "in a hospital for men back from the war. They've lost their minds – can't speak, don't seem to be able to hear anything. They just sit staring at nothing. I read the Bible to them." He paused, as if waiting for Nathan to speak. It was a short time before he did.

"It's terrible thing to see it happen," he said,"and it happens more often than the Army would like people to know. The authorities call it cowardice, the men call it shell shock, but I think it's just sheer terror."

When the two men, still chatting, arrived at Smallbrook Farm, the farmyard was quiet and there appeared to be no one about. Nathan called out loudly for Jenny as they walked through the gate, but there was no answer. That was unusual. Jenny was almost always to be found in or close to the farmyard. He looked around as they walked towards the farmhouse. The door to the small milk shed was closed, so Nathan knew she was not in there; the door to the farmhouse however was wide open. He called again, both for her and for Edward, but still with no response. Glancing anxiously at the vicar, he hurried to the farmhouse door and the two men entered the kitchen together. Neither of them was prepared for what they saw.

Edward Tiley was slumped dead in the bed, blood everywhere from a gunshot wound just behind his right ear. Nathan almost retched when he saw the exit wound on the left side. Reverend Simpkins, noticing the same thing, could not help himself and was violently ill on the floor. Edward's service revolver lay on the floor next to the bed where it had fallen. Of Jenny there was no sign. He looked for guidance at the ashen-faced vicar, who had quickly recovered himself and was now saying a few words over Edward. Then he pulled the blood-sodden sheet up over the dead man's head.

"I think he may have been far more troubled than either you or Jenny believed, Nathan," he said quietly. However, Nathan's thoughts were not with Edward, whose troubles, great though they might have been, were over. They were firmly with Jenny. He nodded absently.

"We need to find Jenny, Reverend," he said. "Edward has no need of us, but she might." The vicar agreed and went to look for her upstairs. Nathan decided to search the farm buildings, at the same time trying to prepare himself for whatever state of mind he might find Jenny in, if indeed he found her at all. He found her in the hay loft.

She was lying face down in the loose hay, her head in her hands. Nathan could hear her sobs as he climbed the ladder. She didn't stir as he stepped into the loft and knelt beside her, but her sobbing became more violent as he took her in his arms and held her tightly to stop her shaking. He didn't try to talk to her for a few minutes, just held her patiently until the fresh bout of sobs died down.

"Jenny? Are you hurt?" he asked gently. There was no reply, only a renewal of the sobbing and shaking. He said no more, only held her quietly until he heard the Reverend Simpkins calling his name.

"It's all right, vicar. She's up here, but in no state to come down. Can you stand being in the kitchen long enough to boil a kettle? I think we all need a strong cup of tea." It was a few minutes before Jenny raised her head from his chest.

"He...he did it front of me," she sobbed. "Is he...is he

dead?"

"Yes, Jenny. He's dead. Are you hurt?" She shook her head. Another short burst of sobbing was followed by her sitting up and trying unsuccessfully to dry her eyes on a handkerchief offered by Nathan. After a few more silent minutes, a voice came up to them from below.

"I've brought some tea," called the vicar. Nathan gave Jenny a reassuring hug and helped her climb down to the barn floor. The vicar had made three large mugs of hot sweet tea, and was sitting on a large wooden box sipping at his as they joined him. Jenny, who'd been unsure whose voice it was she had heard, was surprised to see who it was, but couldn't even give gave him a faint smile of welcome.

"Please accept my condolences, Mrs Tiley," the vicar said. Jenny glanced towards him, nodded in acknowledgement, but still said nothing. She sat on another wooden box, her back to the barn door, and gratefully accepted the tea, cradling the mug in both hands. Neither man could see her face in the shadows thrown by the light coming into the barn from behind her. Nathan wrapped an old blanket around her shoulders before settling himself against the loft ladder.

"Jenny," he began. She looked uncertainly in his direction, still gently sipping her tea. "Can you tell us what happened?" She nodded, but it was some minutes before she began.

"It was horrible," she said quietly, speaking more to her mug than to either Nathan or the vicar. "We were arguing and Eddie was getting more and more angry and nasty about ...

things." She paused, visibly upset. Nathan gave her what he hoped was a reassuring smile.

"Jenny," said the vicar. "Nathan came to me today, presumably with your consent, and explained a little of the circumstances. I'm sorry I didn't get here in time to help Edward, but I'll do all I can now to help you." He placed a hand on her arm, and now received a grateful smile in return. "I presume these 'things' you were arguing about involved Nathan?" Jenny simply nodded once more, but then began to speak again, still quietly into her mug rather than look at Nathan and the vicar.

"He started saying things about Nathan and me and about what he thought we'd been doing. He's been saying things like it since he came back to the farm and met Nathan." Nathan glanced quickly up at her, then returned his gaze to the floor. "Then he wanted me to ... well, he wanted me to do the things to him that he thought I was doing for Nathan. He said he was still my husband and still a man with a man's desires, and if I could let Nathan, then..." She burst out sobbing again, and dropped her half-empty mug to the barn floor as she put her hands over her face. The vicar moved over and put his arm around her, and she buried her face in his shoulder. It was some time before the sobbing ceased again.

"Eddie told me a wife had her duties and when I said 'No' he threatened me with a gun. Vicar, the doctor in Hereford told me he wouldn't be able to ... to do anything down there! But Eddie said I had to try because he had a gun. I didn't know he had a gun – did you Nathan?" Nathan shook his head, feeling like a lead weight had been dropped on him. He couldn't bring himself to say yes. Of course he knew Tiley had a gun. The problem was he'd forgotten to do something about it. He should have taken it away, considering the state of Edward Tiley's mind. "He was waving it around, saying he would shoot me if I didn't get into bed with him but that I deserved shooting anyway for being the whore I was." She glanced at the vicar as she spoke, but he remained impassive apart from the occasional glance at Nathan, who was finding it difficult to restrain his anger. There was another long pause while Jenny prepared herself to go on. Both men remained patient, allowing her all the time she needed.

"He wasn't the Eddie I once knew or that anyone in the village would have known, vicar. He was ranting like a crazy man, and I was so, so scared. But he was right. He was my husband, so I tried to do what he wanted, but nothing happened. Just like the doctor had said. He started crying and screaming and then he pushed me away. I fell and banged my head on the floor." For the first time Nathan noticed a patch of congealed blood in Jenny's hair. "I didn't dare move or even look at him. I'd never heard a man cry the way he cried. Then I heard the bang. It was so loud in the kitchen. I thought he was shooting at me, trying to kill me. Everything went quiet after just the one shot. When I dared to look around at him his eyes were staring straight at me, straight into my soul. They were blaming me, hating me!"

"No my dear, you aren't to blame for this," said the vicar firmly. She buried her head in his shoulder again and Nathan could only just hear her mumbling "But his eyes, his eyes". The vicar stroked the back of her head as if she were a young child woken from a nightmare, a simple action that seemed to give

Jenny a great deal of comfort. "Your husband was a casualty of the war," the vicar continued, still stroking her head. "It was his injuries which led to this tragedy, not anything you did – or didn't do." His voice was soothing and gentle and Nathan agreed with every word. From everything Jenny had told him, the Edward Tiley that came back to Smallbrook from France was a very different man to the Edward Tiley she had married. But however hard he tried, even for Jenny's sake, he couldn't feel any remorse over the man's death, just an anger about how it had happened and what it had done to Jenny.

"When I saw him, just lying there, staring at me, I ran out of the house. I couldn't help myself." Jenny had suddenly started speaking again. "There was so much blood..." Her voice trailed off as she looked down at her dress and with a long low moan, burst into tears again, obviously not having noticed before that it was itself heavily splattered with Edward's blood.

Chapter Twenty-seven

Although reluctant to go back into the farmhouse, Nathan was very conscious of the state of Jenny's dress, and said he would fetch her a clean replacement from her room. He paused by the farmhouse door, took a breath and went in. Crossing the kitchen to open the door to the stairs that had caused so much trouble the day before, Nathan paused again and took in the scene. Edward's body still lay on the bed, covered from view, but something caught Nathan's eye, something which disturbed him, something which wasn't quite right. It was Edward's revolver. He carried on up the stairs and was taking a dress from Jenny's wardrobe when he realised what was wrong, and he hurried back to the kitchen to confirm his suspicions.

The gun was still lying on the floor where it had fallen when Edward died and that was the problem. To have fallen where it did, Edward would have been holding it in his right hand. His missing right hand. According to Jenny, Edward had been waving it around before he pushed her away, so why was it lying on the floor on the right hand side of the bed? He made an instant decision and using his foot, edged the gun around to the other side of the bed, to where it should have fallen. He refused to think about what it might possibly mean and returned to the barn with Jenny's clean dress. She changed into it while the two men turned their backs, and left the blood stained dress lying in the dust of the barn floor.

There were things to be done and the vicar decided it would be for the best if Nathan went to the village to fetch Doctor

Allerby and Constable Lodge, the ageing village policeman while he stayed to comfort Jenny. Nathan and the doctor were the first to arrive back at Smallbrook, in the doctor's small trap, with the constable arriving out of breath a few minutes later on his bicycle. Leaving the two new arrivals to have a short serious-looking conversation, the constable already making notes in his notebook,

Nathan walked across to the barn to wait with Jenny and the vicar. They didn't have long to wait. Constable Lodge, looking very ill at ease at having to deal with such a a violent incident, wanted to talk to Jenny, as Nathan had expected. The policeman began by explaining that he had taken possession of the gun, which would be kept under safe-keeping. Crouched uncomfortably on his haunches, notebook in hand, Constable Lodge looked pale and serious, but tried to put Jenny at ease. She sat next to Reverend Simpkins, who was holding her hands in his.

"It's a bad business, Mrs Tiley, and that's for sure," he started. "I'm very sorry for your loss, especially in these circumstances, but I must ask you some questions about what's happened here at Smallbrook. Can you tell me what happened in the kitchen?" Jenny nodded without looking at him and in what seemed to Nathan to be a very lifeless voice ran through the events of the morning exactly as she had described to him and the vicar. The policeman asked the occasional question, all the while jotting down her words in his notebook.

"Did he seem at all disturbed to you before today, Mrs Tiley?" he asked and before Doctor Allerby could reply in her

208

stead, Constable Lodge held up his hand to quiet him. "I'd rather Mrs Tiley answered, sir." Jenny looked at him blankly. "Was he in his right mind before today, Ma'am?" he repeated.

"No," she answered quietly but firmly. "He wasn't in his right mind and hadn't been since I brought him back to Smallbrook from the hospital."

"And which hospital was that?"

"Hereford General Hospital," she replied.

"And would you remember which doctor was treating him?"

"A Doctor Dougall."

"Thank you for your help, Mrs Tiley. I'm sorry if it's been difficult for you." Replacing his pencil in his pocket, Constable Lodge snapped his notebook shut. The finality of the action prompted Nathan into a question.

"What happens now?" he asked.

"Now?" The policeman looked genuinely confused and thought for a moment or two. "My report will go to my superiors in Exeter, but I can't see there being any further investigation. It all seems straightforward to me."

"Straightforward?" Nathan was pushing to find out what conclusion the constable had come to and what he would be putting into his report. The position of the gun on the kitchen floor, although known only to him, was still troubling him.

"Suicide, sir. Plain and simple. The work of a man out of mind."

"I don't think there's much doubt of that." It was Doctor Allerby who spoke. Standing by quietly, he had keeping a careful eye on Jenny. "Have you finished with Mrs Tiley?" The question was directed at Constable Lodge, who nodded. "Good. I need to talk to her myself." Nobody moved. "Alone, please," he said more firmly. The other three men moved obediently into the farmyard. It was the vicar who spoke first.

"The body will have to be moved," he said. "I'll talk to the undertaker and ask him to come out, but what are to do about Jenny? She can't stay here. We have to find somewhere for her to go, at least until after the funeral." Both Nathan and Constable Lodge agreed with him, but it was Nathan who came up with a suggestion.

"What about the Lamb, with Martha Carter? She'll take good care of Jenny." The other two agreed, and it was suggested to Jenny when Doctor Allerby walked her across from the barn. Nathan was concerned to see her constantly glancing at the kitchen door.

"What about the farm? The cows, the chickens?" she asked.

"I'll look after the farm, Jenny," said Nathan. "There's no need to worry." He thought she seemed vague and distant and looked at Doctor Allerby to see if he'd noticed. The doctor put his hand on Nathan's arm in response to the glance.

"I've given her a little something to help calm her," he said quietly. Nathan smiled gratefully, but said nothing. Raising his voice slightly, the doctor addressed the group. "I'll take Jenny and Nathan to the village in the trap, and Nathan can take her to The Lamb. Then," he added smiling, "I'll be back for you, vicar."

"No need. I'll be fine walking. It's good for the soul." It was the vicar's turn to smile.

"I'll need some things." Jenny's voice, now sounding slightly slurred, brought them back to the gravity of the situation. She looked again at the kitchen door.

"I'll fill a bag for you," Nathan said quickly and Jenny although still a little vague, looked grateful. She certainly didn't want to go into the house herself.

If Joshua Carter was surprised a little later to see Nathan and Jenny enter his empty bar, with Nathan carrying a large bag, he didn't show it.

"Hello, lad. You've been a long time coming for that pint," he said smiling at them both. The smile faded as he noticed how upset and distraught Jenny appeared to be.

"Is Martha out the back?" Nathan asked.

"Aye lad. She's in the kitchen. Where else?" Joshua glanced again at Jenny, a worried look now on his face. "Come on through." as they slipped through behind the bar, he added quietly, for only Nathan to hear, "Is everything alright, lad?"

"Come through with us, Joshua," Nathan replied, just as softly.

"I'll bolt the front door, first, then I'll be right with you," Joshua said, hurrying off to do as he'd said.

Martha was indeed in the kitchen, busy as always, although she never seemed to be anything else. Nathan tapped on the kitchen door, just to let her know there was someone there, and not startle her. She still looked round sharply, as she wasn't expecting anybody. Seeing Nathan, she smiled, wiping her hands on a towel by the sink. The smile changed to a look of surprise as she noticed Jenny standing slightly to one side.

"Come in, come in both of you," she said. As they walked into the kitchen, Joshua appeared behind them, and Martha instinctively knew there was a problem. Gathering her thoughts and wondering what might be wrong, she turned and put the kettle onto the kitchen range and suggested they sit at the table while it boiled. Surprisingly for a publican's wife, a good cup of tea was Martha's answer to most difficulties.

"What's wrong? Nathan? Jenny?" she asked. Then she noticed the bag Nathan had left in the doorway. "What's happened?" She now sounded anxious, and saw for the first time the vagueness in Jenny's eyes. Nathan recounted the day's events, and the kettle was left boiling and ignored on the range as he spoke. Finally Nathan told Joshua and Martha that the vicar had suggested Smallbrook wasn't a suitable place for Jenny at the moment.

"I hoped you'd be good enough to let her stay here for a little while," he finished.

"Of course you can stay, Jenny, for as long as you need to." Nathan was surprised that it was Joshua who replied making the offer, not deferring to his wife for a decision as he usually did. Then, to Martha, who sat smiling at him, he added, "Now, what

212

about a cup of tea before that kettle boils dry?"

Chapter Twenty-eight

Jenny woke with an awful headache, feeling dizzy and nauseous and with no idea of where she was. She was perfectly aware she wasn't in her own bedroom at Smallbrook, but she couldn't remember why. To go along with feeling ill, she also had an almost uncontrollable urge to cry, for no reason that she could think of. It didn't seem to matter though. The bed was warm and comfortable and the pillows soft against the throbbing in her head. She pulled the heavy blankets and counterpane up to her chin and tried to settle back to sleep.

Martha, sitting downstairs quietly for a few minutes while Joshua was cleaning the bar, was startled by the scream from Jenny's room, and it had her rushing upstairs from the kitchen and bursting into the young woman's room without pausing to knock or even consider knocking on the door. Jenny was sitting up in the bed, covers thrown to one side, hair dishevelled, looking hot and flushed and wide-eyed with fright.

"Jenny dear, are you all right? I heard a scream," said Martha, breathless from the unaccustomed dash up the stairs. Jenny looked at her, perplexed.

"Mrs Carter? But what...? Where...?" she stammered, obviously confused. Martha sat on the edge of the bed.

"Jenny, you're at the Lamb. Nathan brought you here yesterday. Everything is all right." With a reassuring smile, she put her arm around the younger woman, who seemed to settle into its security.

"Mrs Carter, I..." Jenny began, but Martha interrupted with another smile.

"It's Martha, not Mrs Carter," she said.

"Martha, I was... It was his eyes, staring at me." Martha knew immediately what the problem was, and tightened her hold around Jenny's shoulders a little.

"It was a dream, Jenny, just a bad dream. Doctor Allerby said you'd have them and he left something to help calm you." She paused, looking at Jenny's distraught face. "I think it would be a good idea for you to have some now." Jenny nodded, willing to follow the advice, tears beginning to flow down her cheeks. Martha reached for a large brown bottle standing on the bedside cabinet and poured a small measure into a glass. Holding the glass out, she continued talking to Jenny. "He said he'd be in to see you later this morning."

"He?"

"Doctor Allerby, Jenny."

"Oh." She drank the medicine and handed the glass back to Martha. "I thought you meant Nathan." She laid her head back on the pillow and looked at Martha, the fear once more on her face. "I don't want to dream of his eyes, Martha."

"I'm sure you won't, not with the doctor's medicine," replied Martha. With Jenny's eyes already starting to look heavy once more, Martha stood, and after a moment's thought, took the glass and the bottle of medicine out of the room with her, closing the door quietly. Jenny was asleep before the latch dropped.

Walking thoughtfully down the stairs, Martha found Joshua waiting anxiously at the bottom, one hand resting on the banister post as if he'd been considering going up.

"Is she all right?"

"Yes, I think so. She's already asleep again. I gave her some of Doctor Allerby's magic potion. Did you hear her scream?" Joshua looked surprised.

"No," he said. "I just saw you dashing up the stairs. Fastest you've moved in many a year," he added, grinning.

"I'm sure it was just a bad dream, something about eyes. The doctor said she'd have them. Hopefully she'll feel a little better when wakes up next time." Joshua raised his eyebrows. He wasn't so sure.

Doctor Allerby was inclined to agree with Joshua. After examining Jenny later in the morning, he had a long chat with Martha and explained that he thought Jenny shouldn't go back to Smallbrook for some time, until her mind was settled. He asked how long she would be able to stay at the Lamb.

"We've already told her and Nathan that she can stay as long as she wants to," Martha replied.

"I'm hoping that what she needs and what she wants turn out to be the same thing," said the doctor. "She needs time to get over this terrible tragedy. I can give her medicine to keep her calm, but I can't change what she thinks about. The one thing I'm sure of is that she mustn't be constantly reminded of it. That's why Smallbrook is no place for her until she's getting over things." He paused for what seemed an interminably long time, giving Martha the unmistakeable impression that he had more to say. She was right. "Martha, about Nathan..." he began.

"What about Nathan?" she said defensively, already thinking she might not like what she was about to hear.

"I don't think it would be a good thing for Jenny to see him..." the doctor said, but he didn't manage to finish what he'd started before Martha angrily interrupted him.

"Not see Nathan? Isn't he the one person who could give her the comfort she needs? Why on earth would you say she shouldn't see him?"

"Martha, don't be angry. At the moment I think Jenny's relationship with Nathan is part of the problem. She needs to be able to cope with what has happened before she can begin to think about her and Nathan."

"Does Jenny know about this?" Martha asked.

"No, I don't think he should be mentioned if it can be avoided."

"I don't like secrets," Martha replied sharply.

"It's for her own good," the doctor said. "Just for a few days, Martha."

"But what can I tell Nathan if he comes to see her? How can I stop him?"

"I'll talk to Nathan and explain that I think she needs time and rest to get over what's happened, possibly until after the funeral. He's a good man, Martha. I'm sure he'll see the sense of it."

"I don't like it," said Martha, "but if you think it's for the best..." She hesitated. "We'll take good care of her here." Doctor Allerby looked relieved, but as he left, Martha couldn't help but think of Nathan. Who was going to take care of him? How would he react to not being able to see Jenny?

Doctor Allerby was true to his word. After calling in on two more patients in the village, both elderly ladies, he made his way out to Smallbrook, slightly reluctantly considering the events of yesterday and the message he was carrying to Nathan. At the farm, everything seemed as it should, with noisy chickens underfoot and the sound of hammering coming from the direction of the barn. The remains of a large bonfire smouldered in the corner of the farmyard and the smell of ashes hung in the air, disappearing as he stopped in the doorway of the barn to be replaced by the very pleasant smell of apples from the still un-stoppered cider casks lined against one wall. He paused a few minutes observing Nathan with a professional eye. He looked fitter and healthier than when he had first returned to the village, the doctor was glad to see. Nathan, becoming aware of someone's presence, turned and was surprised to see Doctor Allerby. He greeted him with a friendly smile.

"Hello Doctor. I wasn't expecting you."

"I've been to see Mrs Tiley this morning," the doctor replied, "and I wanted to talk to you about her." Nathan's stomach lurched a little and a worried look appeared on his face. Had the doctor found out something? Had Jenny said something to him about Edward's death?

219

"Is there a problem? Has something happened?" The doctor smiled and shook his head and Nathan relaxed a little.

"No," he said. "It's just a few thoughts and I thought we might take the chance to talk about you as well."

"Me?" Nathan was puzzled.

"Well you are one of my patients, aren't you?" The doctor smiled again. Nathan suggested they go into the house, where they would be more comfortable sitting in the kitchen. Hesitating only slightly as he recalled the scene in the kitchen from the day before, the doctor followed Nathan across the farmyard. The kitchen was eerily normal. Nathan explained that the bed and all of the bedding had been burned and the remainder of the furniture put back to how it was before Edward's return to the farm.

"That explains the smell of burning in the farmyard," said Doctor Allerby, sitting at the table. Once seated, he reached into his bag, pulled out a brown envelope and laid it on the table between them. Nathan's heart sank a little as he recognised the War Department crest. He didn't need the doctor to tell him what it was about. "It arrived this morning, Nathan," Doctor Allerby said, "so I'll need to ask you some questions about how you feel about your health." Nathan nodded. The army wanted to know if he was fit for a return to duty. Convalescent leave was not an indefinite period away from the uniform.

"I'd managed to forget all about this," he said to the doctor.

"It's taken a long time in coming," replied Doctor Allerby.

"Now, how is your leg holding up?"

"Much stronger than it was when I left the hospital, but I can't walk too fast or too far without it giving way. Other than that, it's fine." He paused, and added with a smile, "How I'd get on marching with a full pack and rifle is another question, though."

"What about sleeping?" the doctor asked.

"Do you mean the dreams?" Doctor Allerby nodded. "Only once, when I found out Edward Tiley was coming back to Smallbrook."

"So you've not been using the tablets?"

"For the past few weeks, yes I have. I couldn't sleep without them."

"A few weeks. Since Edward came back?" Nathan nodded. The doctor wasn't surprised by the answer. He pushed the envelope towards Nathan and gestured for him to read the contents. Nathan unfolded the official letter slowly and read through it. He was surprised that the army, in the shape of one Corporal Arthur Symonds, clerk, was not asking whether Doctor Allerby considered Nathan fit for a return to active service, but fit for duties at the supply depot in Exeter. He glanced up at the doctor.

"Well I can't argue with that, can I? If I can do farm work, I can certainly sit behind a desk and use a pen." He felt empty. This was not a good time for this to be happening. He folded the letter, placed it back in the envelope and handed it to the doctor, who returned it to his bag. "Are you replying to it straight away?"

221

"Yes, I am. My duty is to care for all my patients and I think it would harm Mrs Tiley if she were to learn that you have been called back to the army at this point in time. I also think you're more useful here at Smallbrook than sitting behind a desk, Nathan, but at the best I can only delay things for a month or two. The army will be too busy to notice anything for that amount of time." He hesitated before continuing, a serious look on his face. "I also wanted to talk to you about Mrs Tiley, Nathan." Nathan nodded. "But I think what I'm going to suggest might be quite difficult for you." Again, Nathan felt anxious, but grew a little impatient as he waited for the doctor to continue. "If you agree, I'd like to ask you not to see Mrs Tiley until the funeral."

"Not see her?" Nathan almost exploded. "For God's sake why not?" But mixed in with the anger and shock was slight element of relief. He'd been wondering how to face Jenny when he had such awful suspicions about Edward's death.

"Don't be angry, Nathan. Just hear me out. She needs time to get over what happened yesterday. For better or worse, you're very involved with those events." Watching Nathan carefully, Doctor Allerby was relieved to see his words were having some effect.

"I can understand that," Nathan said, confirming the doctor's thoughts. This would give him a few day's grace in which to get his own thoughts in order, Nathan decided. "If you think it's best for Jenny, then I'll not visit her." Doctor Allerby was a little surprised; he'd been expecting more of an argument.

"Thank you, Nathan. It will only be for a few days," he said, rising from the table and picking up his bag. Nathan remained seated while the doctor let himself out of the kitchen, and it was some time after the doctor had gone that he realised he'd not asked either how Jenny was or how she felt about this arrangement. It didn't enter his mind that she might not even have been told.

Chapter Twenty-nine

As the days passed, Martha was becoming increasingly worried about Jenny and how she was coping with everything. The awful events at Smallbrook had affected her really badly. Despite being well-looked after at the Lamb and shielded as far as possible from all the unpleasant arrangements which had to be made, she'd retreated into herself. The only people she had contact with, apart from Martha and Joshua, were Doctor Allerby, who called on her every day, and Reverend Simpkins, not quite such a frequent visitor.

It was the vicar, having gained the information from Constable Lodge, who told Jenny that the authorities in Exeter had called for a coroner's hearing, explaining to her that it was a mere formality in the case of a suicide. The news had seemed to shock her, so much so that the vicar had called Martha up to Jenny's room. Martha had put the distressed young woman to bed while the vicar went for the doctor. If anything she looked more haunted than ever to the worried Martha. The news, brought a few days later by the constable, that the coroner had unsurprisingly returned a verdict of suicide, had only seemed to rouse her slightly.

Martha was convinced that a little more company might be good for Jenny, someone to talk to other than the doctor and the vicar, both of whom she was coming to believe were keeping something from her about Jenny. Jenny, however, refused all offers of company, even eating her meals in her own room, meals that she was only picking at, not finishing. Martha was also concerned that Jenny was making no attempt to eat breakfast, even refusing the offer. Martha lived by the maxim that breakfast was the most important meal of the day, but Jenny insisted on not having any, and complaining of feeling ill in the mornings because of the medication Doctor Allerby was giving her.

Jenny herself had none of the worries that Martha had that she was becoming too reclusive. She simply didn't want to talk to anybody. In the first days of her stay she had ventured out onto the landing outside her door, intending to go down and sit in the kitchen with Martha. Each time she had stopped at the top of the stairs and hearing voices coming from the bar area, had rushed anxiously back to her room. Since those attempts, most of her time was spent sitting on the wooden chair in her room gazing out of the window to the fields beyond the village and beyond the brook. She'd slightly re-arranged the furniture in the small room to give her this view, although most of the time it meant little to her. It was just a direction in which to look. Her mind was too occupied with thoughts tumbling over each other to absorb what she was seeing in front of her.

Yet if anyone had asked her what she was thinking so deeply about, she wouldn't be able to tell them. It was almost as if it took too much effort to actually concentrate on what she was thinking. It was easier to let her thoughts chase each other around her mind in an incomprehensible torrent. Of Nathan, she only thought occasionally, with a feeling of disappointment and anger at his apparent desertion of her, while Edward haunted her night-time dreams, not her waking mind. But what she felt most of all was a sense of loss and emptiness that she couldn't

226

explain. As a result, the view, lovely as it was, held no real pleasure for her.

And so she sat, hands clasped tightly together in her lap, looking but not seeing and appearing deep in thought without thinking.

Chapter Thirty

George Wilkins was an infrequent visitor to the Lamb, not being a big drinker, but he was always a welcome one. Joshua, interrupted in the age-old publican's task of cleaning glasses, was surprised to find the burly old farmer knocking on the pub door in the early afternoon.

"Afternoon, Joshua," George said.

"George. A surprise to see you," Joshua replied. "A strange time of day for you, but you know you're always welcome. Come on in, and we'll take a half through to the back, if you've a mind?" Joshua stood to one side and ushered his visitor inside, the narrow passage to the bar suddenly becoming quite cramped with the presence of two big men.

"Thanks, Joshua, but it's young Mrs Tiley I'm here to see. I'll be glad of one after I've seen her, though."

"Sounds very business-like, George," Joshua said as they walked along the passage towards the back of the building.

"Social and business, Joshua. A bit of both." The shrewd old farmer was well aware that Joshua was angling to find out the purpose of his visit, but that was to remain firmly between him and Jenny, whatever it was. "To tell the truth, I'm a bit worried about the girl, and she's asked to see me," was all he would admit to. He smiled, noticing the publican's unmistakeable curiosity.

"We're all worried about her, George. She won't come out

of her room." Martha had joined them at the foot of the stairs, the open door of the kitchen filling the air with the fragrant aroma of the meal she and Joshua had just eaten.

"Hello Martha. I'm glad she's in good hands," said George.

"She's expecting you, George," said Martha, which brought a frown to Joshua's face, as he certainly hadn't known. "First room on the left at the top of the stairs." She stood with Joshua and watched the farmer go on up, before both of them went into the kitchen.

Jenny and George were closeted together for some time upstairs, and it was almost an hour later that George came back downstairs and accepted Joshua's earlier offer of half a pint of the publican's own recipe beer. If Joshua was still hoping to find out why Jenny wanted to the farmer, he was disappointed. The reason for the visit wasn't discussed. It was plain however that George Wilkins was certainly worried about Jenny.

"She's in a bad way," he said. "Not like herself at all," he added.

"The doctor's seeing her every day," said Martha. "He says it's shock and it will take time for her to recover, but I really don't know." Both men were inclined to agree with her. Jenny's mind seemed to have become unbalanced, and that might need more than a village doctor. The conversation meandered for a short while.

"How's Nathan doing out at Smallbrook, George? We haven't seen him since the day he turned up on our doorstep with Jenny." It was Joshua who asked the question.

"Nathan? He's doing fine. Make a good farmer someday if he sticks at it. I saw him a couple of days ago, and he wasn't particularly talkative, which is unlike him. I was surprised when he told me he'd not left Smallbrook since the day that Tiley killed himself."

"No," said Martha. "No one's seen him in the village. I just hope he's alright." She looked as concerned as she sounded.

If anyone had asked Nathan how he was doing, he would have said that yes, he was fine, because he wouldn't dream of saying anything else, but he was a troubled man. He'd thrown himself into a myriad of tasks around the farm, deliberately tiring himself, but still needing the tablets given him by Doctor Allerby to help him sleep a dreamless sleep. It was after he woke each morning that the troublesome thoughts began, staying with him no matter how hard he worked. Knowing that he loved Jenny deeply, more deeply than he'd felt anything, he was being torn apart by conflict. If he loved her as much as he thought, no, he knew he did - she was on his mind every waking moment, wanting to hold her close, to comfort her, to run his fingers through her hair – then he shouldn't have any doubts or suspicions or worries about her at all. But he did. Just one. A very big one. He was convinced that Edward Tiley couldn't possibly have pulled the trigger on the revolver he was supposed to have used to kill himself.

Chapter Thirty-one

The weather was changing, with forlorn grey rain-bearing clouds dominating the sky, reflecting the atmosphere of Dalton Combe. The events at Smallbrook Farm had cast a pall of depression over the village and the villagers alike. Scandal and apparent misdeeds were one thing, and were fair game for gossip and tittle-tattle, but it was a step too far to be caught talking in public about such a tragedy. As a consequence, an air of gloom had enveloped everybody.

Even Reverend Simpkins couldn't escape this feeling. He felt strongly that Edward Tiley's death was a tragedy that need not have happened, and he felt some responsibility for not having been able to prevent it. Each morning since he'd arrived in the little village, he liked to spend some time alone in the church, simply sitting and thinking, but this morning the church had taken on a chilly air, and with Edward Tiley's funeral later in the day, his thoughts had been filled with the tragedy at Smallbrook. He'd been to see Jenny at the Lamb, to offer what solace and support he could and had been surprised each time at the change in her. Withdrawn, vague and hardly speaking, she was nothing like the person he'd known just weeks before. Martha, had persuaded him into a cup of tea on his last visit, along with a piece of cake that was so delicious it was almost sinful. She'd then told him of her worries about the younger woman. And then of course there was Nathan, who he'd not seen since the day of the tragedy. Still looking after Smallbrook, Nathan hadn't visited Jenny, which had surprised him, but neither had Jenny asked about Nathan, which had surprised him even more. It was very strange and very sad. Standing up from his rather uncomfortable seat in the front pew, and resolving once again to make his sermons shorter, he stepped into the main aisle of the church. Respectfully inclining his head towards the altar and the cross, he murmured a short prayer of thanks for this short time alone with God, and then turned and walked away towards the church door.

Even with the grey cloud-filled sky and no sign of the sun, it was much brighter outside than it had been inside the church and the vicar squinted for a few moments as his eyes adjusted to the light. He felt a few drops of rain and immediately regretted not having taken his housekeeper's advice and brought a coat with him. Hearing the sound of some activity from behind the church, he rounded the east end of the building to enter the north side of the churchyard, where Harry Mason and a younger man he didn't recognise were finishing off work on the grave to be used later for Edward Tiley.

This area of the churchyard always saddened him. Burials in the northern side of Dalton Combe churchyard were not common. Traditionally, the ground to the north of a church was unconsecrated ground, used only for the burials of paupers, unbaptised children, suicides and murderers. Long before Reverend Simpkins had been ordained, in fact even before the old queen had come to the throne, those rules had been revoked by law, and these types of burials were now allowed in consecrated ground, but usually to the north of the church. It was still considered by many people including the people of Dalton Combe that a burial to the north carried a certain stigma with it.

The vicar sighed as he watched the two men at work. The Diocesan office had brought pressure to bear for this particular funeral to be in the north part of the churchyard. Noticing him the two men, both in shirtsleeves and braces, straightened up, so he walked across to them.

"Mornin' vicar," said Harry, quite cheerfully considering the type of work he was doing.

"Good morning, Harry. How's it going?" Reverend Simpkins gestured towards the grave.

"Fine vicar. It'll be ready for this afternoon." With a few more spots of rain falling, Harry added "and it looks as if the weather's fixing to give us a proper damp one as well." Looking skywards, the vicar agreed. A gloomy funeral was always made worse by wet weather, although he was also aware that there were people who considered wet weather to be only fitting for a funeral.

"And who is this?" he asked Harry, turning towards the young man, who had doffed his cap deferentially to the clergyman.

"This is my grandson, young Maurice. You remember I told you his ma and pa were killed in the Zeppelin raids last year?" The vicar nodded.

"Golders Green, wasn't it?" he said to the young man.

"Yes, in September. Not many people were killed. I guess my ma and pa were just unlucky," said Maurice.

"He's off to the army," said Harry proudly, "and he's come

to see me and his grandma before he goes." The vicar was surprised. The young man didn't look old enough to shave, let alone go off and fight.

"Good luck to you, Maurice," he said, "and may God be with you."

"I certainly hope He is, vicar," replied Maurice. Then Reverend Simpkins turned to Harry.

"Come and see me after the funeral for your fee, Harry. Ill be in the vestry." There was a pause and Reverend Simpkins could see a confusion of thoughts pass over the old man's face.

" If Missus Tiley's payin', I'd rather not take anything if it's alright by you vicar," the old man said.

"She isn't paying, Harry, but thank you for your kind thought. You'll get your fee." Harry thanked him and the vicar walked slowly away in the direction of the rectory, his thoughts turning back to Jenny Tiley and how she was likely to be affected by the funeral service.

He was both surprised and relieved to find that she handled it very well, but it was obvious that her mind was elsewhere and she seemed to be simply going through the motions. Despite constant reassurance from Reverend Simpkins that the whole village sympathised with her, there had been few people in the church for the service and Jenny inevitably took this as a judgement against herself. Edward was a suicide and this went against the beliefs of the villagers, and Jenny in her despair, was convinced that they held her to blame for this crime against God. Besides the vicar, the undertaker and the pallbearers provided by the undertaker, the only people in the church were Jenny, Nathan and Martha, who was there to give some support to Jenny. As Nathan was present, Martha had returned quickly to the pub after the burial, in an attempt to give the two young people a little time together.

With Martha gone, Jenny stood quietly at the graveside, looking down at the still uncovered coffin, lost in thought. Nathan stood next to her, watching her closely and holding an umbrella over both of them to shield them from the grey drizzle which had increased in intensity since the few drops of the morning. She seemed completely unaware of Nathan, the rain or even the few drops which occasionally ran down her neck. The only other person at the graveside was the vicar, sheltering under his own umbrella and it was he who broke what was becoming an uncomfortable silence.

"I think we should get indoors out of this rain, don't you?" he said. Jenny didn't move until Nathan gently touched her arm. With a look that stunned him in its complete lack of recognition, she walked away into the rain. Nathan thanked Reverend Simpkins for the service and hurried after her with the umbrella. Reverend Simpkins watched them both go with a sorrowful look on his face, and then made his way into the church to change from his damp robes in the vestry.

Nathan caught up with Jenny at the lych-gate and reached out to take her arm. With a sharp look she pulled it away from his touch.

"Jenny," he said, "at least take the umbrella." She stopped and looked at him, her eyes distant and unfocussed. Shocked, he heard her thank him almost formally for coming to the service, and then, still not having taken the umbrella he offered, she walked quickly off down the lane towards the village.

Chapter Thirty-two

Nathan wasn't sure how long he'd been sitting on the cold stone seat, his head against the coffin rest which split the old lych-gate in two, before he heard footsteps on the path coming from the church. His thoughts were all for Jenny, and they left him feeling desolate and lonely. She'd treated him like a stranger. The rain continued to fall, a persistent flow, but inside his dry shelter, he didn't even bother to look up when the footsteps grew close and finally stopped. A hand rested on his shoulder and he looked up to see the vicar standing anxiously over him.

"Nathan, what are you doing sitting here? As my mother used to say, you'll catch your death of cold," he said. Consumed by small tasks around the church, it had been a long time since he'd gone in to change his clothes and he was concerned to see Nathan had been sitting there that long. "Let's get down to the rectory for a hot drink. I've got an umbrella here with me." He encouraged Nathan to stand and they both ventured out into the rain. Not a word was spoken between them as they walked and they were both more than glad to get out of the rain by the time they reached the vicar's home and the vicar arranged with his housekeeper for tea and toast before he'd even removed his coat. The two men then retired to the vicar's overcrowded and untidy study, where a small fire welcomed them burning brightly in the grate.

They sat quietly waiting for their refreshments, Nathan particularly glad of the warmth of the fire. The tea and hot buttered toast was promptly provided by Mrs Nesbitt, the vicar's housekeeper and the vicar told her to get off home for the day.

"I don't know what I'd do without you, Mrs Nesbitt," he added, much to her discomfort. Like most of the women in the village, she was very uncomfortable with compliments, no matter who they came from or how they were phrased. She closed the door softly and the two men were left alone, with the vicar pouring tea for them both. It was also left to the vicar to open the conversation, knowing without having to ask the cause of Nathan's low mood.

"She's a very sick woman, Nathan. Her mind is definitely unbalanced at the moment," he began. "But she is a strong woman. I'm sure all she needs is time."

"It was a shock seeing her," said Nathan. "I haven't seen her since the day Edward died. Earlier on, it was like she didn't know me, vicar. She even thanked me for coming to the funeral as if I was someone she didn't know." His concern for Jenny was obvious as he spoke, but so was the undeniable fact that he'd been deeply hurt by Jenny's behaviour. "What can I do?" he asked quietly, the helplessness clear in his voice. There was a long pause as the vicar seemed to consider his answer, hands clasped together almost in an attitude of prayer. Nathan, for his part, gazed into the flames of the small fire which was putting up a brave fight against the chill and damp weather outside. The silence, comfortable though it was, seemed endless, and after a quick glance at the vicar, Nathan thought the older man may have gone to sleep in the cosy warmth of the room.

"I don't know, Nathan" the vicar said sadly. "She needs time and support if she's to recover." Nathan almost pounced on the vicar's words.

"That's what Doctor Allerby said, but how can I support her if I don't see her?" The vicar suddenly understood why Jenny hadn't seen Nathan in the past two weeks.

"This is difficult, Nathan, because you're part of her problem, or at least your feelings for each other are," the vicar said gently without opening his eyes, aware that his words had the possibility of further upsetting Nathan, but not knowing Doctor Allerby had told him almost the same thing. The vicar's comments struck Nathan like a knife. "She has feelings for you which increase her sense of guilt over the death of her husband."

"But it was suicide." Reverend Simpkins didn't reply for what seemed like a long time to Nathan.

"Jenny blames herself," he said simply. "All she will say is that it was her fault."

"How can it be her fault? The coroner and the police said he killed himself." Nathan felt very defensive for Jenny, despite his own doubts.

"Yes, they did, didn't they? But it's not what Jenny says. She insists she killed him," replied the vicar. Nathan looked at the vicar, shaking his head in puzzlement.

"How can she possibly believe that?" he found himself saying, more heatedly than he'd intended. Reverend Simpkins put up a placating hand.

"Guilt, whether real or imagined is a powerful emotion," he said. "It can seriously affect the mind, and seems to have done just that with Jenny." Nathan jumped on the vicar's last words.

"Real? Are you saying you think she did it?" he said sharply, not noticing his tone in his anxiety. Reverend Simpkins shook his head.

"No, no. Not at all. I was just talking about guilt." He was puzzled by Nathan's reaction, but put it down to his worry about Jenny.

"You've talked to her about this?" Nathan was worried about what Jenny might have said.

"Yes I have. She was very open with me, and although I think she'd be unhappy if she knew I was telling you." Despite himself, Nathan felt himself colour up a little as the vicar opened his eyes and looked directly at him. It was as if the older man had reached a decision. "I feel you should know something," he said after another pause, still looking disconcertingly and directly into the younger man's eyes.

"What?" Nathan didn't mean his tone to be sharp. "Just stay out of her way until she forgets me?" There was a long worrying pause before the vicar spoke again.

"No, Nathan, it's not that." Nathan had a quick burst of hope as the vicar said those particular words, but the tone of the older man's voice gave him cause for concern. The vicar sounded genuinely sorry about something.

"It seems that Jenny is planning on leaving Dalton Combe."

"Leaving? When? What about the farm?" This was worse than Nathan had imagined. A long pause gave Nathan his answer before the vicar actually spoke and a multitude of arguments rose up in Nathan's mind as to why this shouldn't happen, but he stayed quiet, knowing them all to be futile if Jenny's mind was made up.

"She's already spoken to George Wilkins and ended her tenancy of Smallbrook."

"But I'm looking after Smallbrook for her, vicar," he began and Reverend Simpkins nodded. It had been his idea. "When will all this be happening?"

"Very soon, I believe." After another pause, where Nathan struggled once more to gather his thoughts, the vicar asked, quite simply "Would you like another cup of tea, Nathan? This must have come as a bit of a shock." Although he felt like something a lot stronger than tea, Nathan nodded, if only to gain a little more time to think.

But all he could think of was that Jenny obviously regretted their relationship and how devastated he felt about that. They'd had a chance of real happiness, or so he had thought, and now that was gone. And all because of Edward Tiley. How he hated that man. Then the realisation hit him that if Jenny didn't want him, there was nothing to keep him in Dalton Combe either.

"I should leave," he said, far too abruptly, as the vicar handed him the cup he'd refilled with tea.

"Leave?" asked Reverend Simpkins, unsure of what Nathan meant, and surprised at the force of his comment.

"Yes, leave. Leave Smallbrook Farm. Leave Dalton Combe." The vicar looked long and hard at the young man and

243

could see the deep unhappiness now showing on his face and especially in his eyes.

"I remember telling my father I wanted to enter the church. He was a craftsman, a blacksmith, who always thoroughly thought through every decision he made. He gave me his backing, but told me to take my time, to be confident that I'd made the right decision. His favourite piece of advice to me was 'Act in haste, repent at leisure' and I think that it's a valuable piece of advice for you right now." He paused, and noticed thankfully that Nathan seemed to be listening closely. "Don't do anything rash that you may come to regret, Nathan."

"There's nothing to keep me here now, Vicar," Nathan said quietly, aware that he might be sounding a little petulant and foolish, but not really caring too much. It didn't matter. Jenny simply didn't want anything to do with him and that was what did matter to him. There was another long pause, and the vicar looked at him quizzically. He needed to change the subject, to give Nathan something different to think about for a few minutes.

"Why did you come back here, Nathan?"

"Come back? I don't understand." Nathan was taken by surprise by the change of direction in their conversation.

"Back to Dalton Combe, I meant," the vicar explained.

"I don't really know. I've no family here now, but the only roots I have are in this village." Nathan thought for a few moments before carrying on. "I suppose I wanted to see if coming back here might help to put the war out of my mind." After a few moments and a sip of tea, Reverend Simpkins spoke again.

"Did it help you forget?"

"It's taken away some of the horror, but I'll never forget," Nathan said. "I don't think anyone who was there will. But I did think I'd been given a chance at happiness for the future," he added quietly and the vicar realised it would be futile not to go along with Nathan bringing the subject back to what was upsetting him.

"With Jenny?" the vicar asked gently.

"Yes. It seemed so good, vicar, so good that I should have known it could never have lasted, I suppose," he added in a defeated tone of voice. The vicar looked sympathetically at the young man, who by his tone and demeanour seemed, in the space of their conversation, to have given up hope.

"It's wrong to think that happiness won't come again, Nathan. None of us knows what's around life's corners or what God has planned for us." He stopped and laughed. "Now I sound like a preacher," he said. He was pleased to see a slight smile, albeit fleeting, on Nathan's face. They both finished their tea in silence.

"Where will you go, Nathan?"

"I'll catch the local train to Exeter, and then wherever the army sends me." Nathan replied. "One place is as good as another." Again the vicar noted the dejected tone in Nathan's voice.

No one saw Nathan leave. He'd gone directly to Doctor

Allerby's on leaving the rectory to have the doctor write a letter for him and then had returned to Smallbrook. After a poor night's sleep, it hadn't taken him long to pack his few belongings – an army life had taught him to travel light. He left the farm secure, and was gone in the early morning light.

Chapter Thirty-three

Martha, washing up the breakfast plates in the kitchen of the Lamb, was lost in a daydream as Joshua burst into the room, calling her name and startling her so much she almost dropped a plate.

"What is it Joshua? You're crashing around like a bull in a china shop," she said, smiling.

"It's Nathan," he said to her excitedly. "He's gone. Left Smallbrook. Left the village."

"Where's he gone?" she asked. "Does anyone know? He didn't even say goodbye." Joshua shook his head as the questions poured from his wife.

"Young Jack Evans has just come running back from Smallbrook on his way to Manor Farm with a note. He told me when I met him down by the brook." He paused, with a quick anxious glance towards the kitchen door and the stairs. "'He said the farm was all locked up, with no one around. The cows were waiting to be milked, the chickens hadn't been fed and there was a note stuck to the door."

"Could it be for a short visit somewhere?" Martha asked quietly. Joshua shook his head again.

"Leaving without telling anyone? I don't think so, Martha. I think he's gone for good."

"Surely not. Not without telling us. Not without telling Jenny." Martha couldn't quite believe Nathan would do something like that. She sat at the freshly scrubbed kitchen table and put her head in her hands for a few moments. Looking at Joshua over the tips of her fingers she said quietly "How on earth are we going to tell Jenny?" she asked quietly. A big sigh left her lips. If she'd been a cursing type of woman she thought to herself, at that very moment the name of Nathan Holt would have been cursed up hill and down dale. As she wasn't, she gave her husband a weak smile, left the kitchen without saying anything more and made her way up the stairs to Jenny's bedroom, tapping gently on the door. Getting no answer, she knocked a little louder and then went in anyway.

Jenny was sitting where she so often found her, on her little wooden chair gazing distractedly out of the window. She didn't even notice Martha enter the room.

"Jenny," Martha said quietly, repeating herself a little more loudly when Jenny didn't respond to her name and moving around between her and the window. The younger woman looked up.

"Yes?" she said gently. Martha, having got the younger woman's attention, moved and sat on the bed. Jenny resumed looking out of the window, but obviously listening.

"I've got some news for you, Jenny. Some bad news," Martha said. Jenny didn't respond, so Martha carried on, speaking gently, almost as if to a child. "It's about Nathan." Still no reaction from Jenny. Martha persevered, convinced Jenny was still listening. "He's left Smallbrook, Jenny. At the moment, no-one knows where he's gone." Jenny showed no reaction to Martha's words, but her mind was whirling. Nathan was gone!

248

With her husband – she still couldn't think of Edward in any other way – dead and buried, she was on her own again. Completely on her own.

Tears came unbidden and she continued to look out of the window through watery eyes. It was ridiculous. She didn't want to cry. She was leaving Dalton Combe herself. Nathan, like Edward, was now part of a past she had to put behind her, but now he was gone, she missed him. She had cut him off, pushed him away, she knew that, but still he had stayed at Smallbrook, looking after the farm for her, even though she had not asked. But he hadn't come to see her. Not even a message. Nothing. Until now. She wasn't ready for this, hadn't prepared herself for the possibility of him leaving, hadn't expected it at all. The short time she'd had with Nathan had also been unexpected, but very, very happy. She felt a sense of loss at his departure, much stronger than that she'd felt at Edward's death. She felt regret.

As these thoughts and more tumbled over and over in her mind, matching the slow progress of tears down her cheeks, she continued to sit and gaze vacantly out of the window. The already grey day outside turned to rain in sympathy with her. She unconsciously moved her hands from her lap and placed them on her stomach.

"Jenny, are you all right?" Martha was worried by the silent tears. She rose and standing behind her, put her hands on the young woman's shoulders. Jenny leant back into her for a few moments and then stood herself. Before she really knew what was happening she found herself wrapped in the older woman's arms, sobbing loudly, while Martha comforted her. When Jenny had calmed a little, Martha sat her on the bed, and positioned herself next to her. "Oh, Jenny," was all Martha could find to say while she stroked Jenny's head comfortingly.

Jenny wiped away the tears. Suddenly she felt the need to talk and once she started she found she couldn't stop. Martha sat with her arm around her, providing a sympathetic ear. It had been a very long time since Jenny had been able to pour her heart out to anyone, and from Martha's point of view, it seemed that the young woman had too much bottled up inside her, and her heart went out to her. She finally persuaded Jenny to come downstairs to "have a nice cup o' tea" as she put it and helped her freshen up a bit. Meeting Joshua at the foot of the stairs, Martha asked him to fetch a small brandy for Jenny, who although not keen on drinking, swallowed it as instructed, feeling the warmth of the alcohol course through her. A cup of tea quickly followed, and it seemed to Martha that Jenny was calmer and had pulled herself together a little. Joshua sensed it was time for him to make himself scarce.

"I'll have to decide what to do," Jenny suddenly said to Martha, breaking a lengthening and uncomfortable silence. Martha raised her eyebrows a little.

"I thought you had decided, what with giving up Smallbrook."

"I had to be rid of that farm. I couldn't live there any more. But I didn't think about afterwards."

"Or what Nathan might do," Martha added. Jenny didn't know whether to shake her head or nod. Tears were close again.

"Were you hoping that there would be some future for you and Nathan?" Martha asked sympathetically, correctly judging the look on Jenny's face.

"Yes. No. Yes. Oh I don't know, Martha. It was such a short time, and I was happy. I'd grieved for my husband and then Nathan came along. Don't think badly of me, I didn't intend anything to happen, but when it did – well, it was lovely. Nathan is such a nice person. Finding out about Eddie spoiled it all. It's all my fault, Martha, Eddie being dead, and Nathan leaving like this. It's all my fault." The tears started again, slowly. Martha felt helpless. "I wanted Nathan, Martha. I was so happy," Jenny continued after a short silence. "I wanted him so much and I drove him away because I didn't tell him."

The short conversation soon lapsed into silence, with Martha seeing an all too familiar vacant expression re-appear on Jenny's face before she once more retreated to her room, cheeks still slightly aglow from the brandy. Martha had briefly hoped that the outburst from Jenny might be the first step in her 'recovering her wits' as Joshua had good-naturedly put it a few days before, but she quickly realised this was not to be the case. When Jenny refused some slices of bread and jam that Martha had prepared for her and taken to her room, Martha sent Joshua for Doctor Allerby whose visit seemed longer than usual.

"Doctor, about the medicine Jenny's taking," Martha began.

"Is there a problem?" he interrupted. "Jenny hasn't said anything."

"She keeps telling me it's the reason she's not eating.

She's says she's waking up feeling sick every day."

"Oh, her appetite. Don't worry about that, Martha. She should have it back soon enough." He sounded confident.

"Don't you think it's time she saw one of them doctors that are trained to deal with people like her?" Joshua asked, his concern for Jenny obvious.

"What, in the county asylum, with all the lunatics? What are you thinking of?" Doctor Allerby retorted angrily and very unexpectedly. "The last thing she needs is to be carted off like some madwoman. Especially now," he added.

"That's not what I meant," said Joshua. "I just thought..."

"She needs care and kindness, Joshua, not electric shocks or freezing cold baths." The doctor sounded a little more calm, and looked to Martha for support. The idea of an asylum shocked her, and she was sure that it wasn't what Joshua meant, but she was equally sure Jenny needed more than just something to help her sleep. She didn't get to voice her opinion before Doctor Allerby continued, taking her silence for agreement. "I'm sure all she needs is a few more days," he added in his former confident tone and with that he'd left them looking at each other, both unsure as to why he'd reacted so angrily.

During the night, Martha took it on herself to check on Jenny in light of the news she'd given her that day but she was frightened to find that Jenny wasn't in her room. Rushing downstairs, she found the back door to the pub unlocked and Jenny standing outside in the rain in her nightdress, soaked to the skin, staring up at the sky, although nothing was to be seen but clouds.

Once she had Jenny dry and warm and back in bed, she returned to her own bed, to the snoring Joshua who she'd not woken up, resolving that it might not be a bad thing if the two of them were to keep more of an eye on Jenny if they could manage it.

Chapter Thirty-four

"Bloody foxes!" George Wilkins' angry tone as he crashed through the door at Manor Farm caused his wife to come rushing anxiously down the stairs to see what was wrong. "They're nothing but damned pests!" he continued.

"What's happened?" she asked him. He was already rooting noisily around in the walk-in cupboard where he kept his shotgun.

"Chickens! That's what happened!" His voice was slightly muffled from inside the cupboard. "A fox has got in amongst 'em." he emerged from the cupboard still red in the face with temper but clutching a shotgun and a box of shotgun shells. Even though only the two of them lived in the old rambling house, he was adamant about never having the gun loaded until it had been taken outside. "Whole lot of 'em killed. Ripped to pieces. Feathers everywhere. Why the bloody things can't just take what they need to eat I'll never know. Why kill all of 'em unless it's just for fun? Bloody vermin!"

"But beautiful vermin," his wife said, goading him a little. She was used to how quickly George's tempers came and went.

"Old Reynard won't be so beautiful by the time I've finished with him," George muttered.

"How did we not hear anything?" his wife asked, patting him on the arm.

"I don't know," said George, now starting to relax a little. "I didn't even hear the dogs, and if they're going deaf and didn't hear anything I might as well put a bullet in them as well."

"George, you'll do no such thing," she said firmly, despite knowing full well that he wouldn't.

For the past few months, foxes had seemed to be running free in the area, probably from a family group, George thought to himself. The hunt from nearby Dalton Magna hadn't ridden to hounds since the beginning of the war and the foxes were taking advantage. They seemed to have a new-found confidence. Foxes, he well knew, were territorial animals and although he was well aware that killing one fox wouldn't solve the problem, as another would probably quickly move in take its place especially if the food supply was good, George was determined that before the day was out there would be at least one less fox to bother him for the time being.

"I'll have to go out and see if I can get one of the blighters. With young Holt gone from Smallbrook, the birds there could be in danger."

"Do you have to go today? Just look at the weather out there." It was indeed raining heavily.

"A drop of rain won't stop the foxes, will it? And who could I ask to go in my place? Young Jack Evans? His granddad John with his bad chest? No, it's got to be me."

"What about Harry Mason's young grandson? He's staying with Harry at the moment."

"What's his name? Maurice, isn't it?" She nodded. "No, that young man's going to be seeing more than enough of guns – and it would take too long to tell him where to find them," he added. His wife smiled. What George wasn't saying was that he wouldn't have trusted his precious shotgun to any of them anyway.

Chapter Thirty-five

Smallbrook was quiet, deserted and gloomy in the rain and Jenny didn't know how she came to be there. She didn't remember walking there, nor did she remember even leaving her room at the Lamb, but there she was, and the familiar farmyard entrance drew her in. Even though she was cold and soaking wet, she hadn't noticed the rain. It had rained all the way from the village, leaving her clothes and hair sodden, both clinging to her. The thought of putting on a coat or hat had never entered her mind.

It was muddy and slippery as she walked across the farmyard towards the door of the house, which she was surprised to find locked. She tried the handle again and again, even though a little voice was telling her she shouldn't go in, but she didn't know why. Jenny found it curious that the door was locked, as she couldn't remember locking it and what was more, couldn't think what she might possibly have done with the key, but she shrugged and turned instead to walk across to the cowshed, looking for the cows. Did they need milking? She would check, but she didn't think so. They would be milling around the lower gate to the farmyard and making an awful noise. Anyway, it was something Nathan would have taken care of. Where was Nathan? She couldn't hear him, but she knew he must be around somewhere.

There were no cows in the cowshed, but the chickens and other fowl were still in their pens. She let them out and and watched as they scattered noisily around the farmyard, scratching for food. Then she wondered idly where Nathan was again, and why he hadn't let them out. She was worried about Nathan. Where could he be? And as she stood wondering, still it rained. There is nothing so dreary and even soul-destroying as November rain, but this particular day it was beyond her notice. Grey skies, cold weather, leafless trees and hedges, empty fields and the constant drizzle, soaking everything, all meant nothing to her.

Eddie. Why, standing in the middle of the farmyard did his name pop into her head? Eddie, the man she had loved, the man who'd died on some muddy battlefield somewhere in France. Tears began a slow descent of her cheeks, blending and becoming indistinguishable from the raindrops. Not like that other Eddie, the one who'd come back from the dead. He had not been a nice man. There had been nothing to like about him. The tears stopped, but the rain continued. It really was weather to be avoided, weather to be shut outside and watched through windows of a warm house with a roaring fire at your back.

She looked around. Perhaps Nathan might be in the barn or the hayloft and the thought of the hayloft brought a gentle smile to her wet face. The barn doors were open, so she went in. It was dark and gloomy, with no light entering from the grey wet day outside, but she always kept a lamp and matches at hand near the door. She lit the lamp and held it up in front of her, casting unusually shaped flickering shadows all over the barn walls. No sign of Nathan. Where was he? She called his name. No reply. An unbidden thought crept into her mind. Had he gone somewhere without telling her? Was that why the farm was so quiet? She shook her head to try to rid herself of this unpleasant idea and tried to convince herself he was playing some sort of game of hide-and-seek with her. She called his name again. Still no reply. The unwelcome thought that he'd gone somewhere wouldn't go away. Or was it that he was making hard for her to find him?

Where could he be hiding? Obviously somewhere he could step out and take her in his arms and hold her tightly. She could almost feel the strength of his arms around her when she suddenly thought of the hayloft. Of course. That was the place where they had first ... first been together. Before that other Eddie came back. She smiled again. Yes, that would be where he was hiding.

The ladder to the upper floor was behind where she was standing, and she stepped onto it quite gingerly; her shoes were still covered in slippery mud from the farmyard. Her foot slipped, so she kicked off her shoes, noticing they landed near a small pile of stained cloth of some sort. Then she set off more confidently up the ladder in her bare feet, holding the lantern above her head in one hand as she climbed and tightly onto the ladder with the other. When she reached the top, she placed the lamp carefully on the edge to one side, and clambered into the hayloft.

"Nathan! Are you here, Nathan?" She was still convinced that he was playing games with her. There was no answer. "Nathan!" she called. "Come out here and stop hiding!" Still no answer. She began to doubt that he was there and feeling a little scared, anxiety started to creep into her voice. "Nathan? Please, Nathan?" She sat down with a bump on some hay, and put her head in her hands. And remembered. He was gone. Nathan was gone. Tears started again, quickly turning to wild sobbing. A fresh outburst came when she thought of his strong arms around her in this very hayloft on a hot late summer afternoon. Her mind began to drift along more pleasant thoughts of time with him.

She was not asleep for long; the lamp was still burning brightly when she woke, but only partially lighting the roof space. She didn't at first know where she was, but with a shiver became very aware of being cold and damp, her wet clothes uncomfortable and confused as to how she got there. Standing, and shivering again, she looked around for her coat, but couldn't find one. There was an old blanket downstairs she remembered and that would be perfect to use to warm herself up and to wrap herself in. Shivering again, she stooped to pick up the lamp and found herself staring into a pair of sparkling bright eyes, which were blinking behind a set of long whiskers. It wasn't the first time she'd seen a rat, but she was shocked at its proximity to her face, and screamed, stepping back in alarm. Her hand caught the handle of the lamp and she stepped carefully onto the ladder, not for one second looking away from the rat as she began to descend. The sound of a gunshot in the near distance startled her a little but startled the rat much more and it leapt at her in fright, its sharp claws catching in her cheeks. This time Jenny screamed more loudly with the pain and lost her balance on the ladder as she attempted to knock the rat away. The lamp fell from her grip and went tumbling to the barn floor below where it smashed, splashing oil and flame all around. The dry hay started to burn immediately. Horrified, Jenny fell. Hitting the ground hard, she was unconscious as the fire began to take hold.

Chapter Thirty-six

Walking away from a warm Manor Farm and into the rain reignited George Wilkins' temper towards foxes. There were of course those who had to be out in this weather, morose and uncomfortable though they might be, but being out today was George's own choice. The copse on the hill overlooking Smallbrook was the site of the den, and where he knew the foxes were to be found. He entered the copse with only a casual glance down the hill at the deserted farm, stepping out of the rain and into the relative shelter of the trees where he settled down, gun at the ready, to wait quietly for some sign of his prey.

As is natural when waiting, his thoughts began to wander from the issue at hand, even though his gaze remained steady. He wasn't going to miss any opportunity to make the fox pay for his temerity in killing all of those chickens. It was Smallbrook on his mind. He'd half expected Jenny Tiley to give up the farm, after all her husband, out of his mind though he might have been, had killed himself in the kitchen. On hearing Jenny's decision, George had hoped Nathan Holt might take on the farm and was confident the young man had the right attitude and would be able to make a real go of it. He hadn't thought for one minute that Jenny leaving Dalton Combe might be enough to make Nathan want to go as well. And that left him with the problem of what to do about Smallbrook.

Then the fox appeared in the gloom and even George, with all his comments about pests and vermin, had to admit the beauty of the animal as it cautiously approached its den, nose in the air for the scent of danger. Slightly bedraggled as it was from the weather, it was a fine specimen, a large male with a magnificent brush dangling damply behind it. George sighed, raised the shotgun and pulled the trigger, the sound of the gun shattering the silence and echoing around the trees. The animal dropped to the ground instantly.

George straightened himself up gingerly. He'd been in the same position too long for a man of his age, he thought. Standing over the dead animal, he felt little satisfaction from his actions, just the feeling of an unavoidable chore finished. Then, breaking the spell of the moment, he turned away and took the empty cartridges from the shotgun, dropping them into his pocket.

Slipping and sliding and then cursing and swearing when he actually fell over once, cracking his knee painfully against a fallen branch, he finally emerged once more from the copse and saw Smallbrook below him with smoke coming from the barn. His running days long behind him, he hurried down the hill and across the rough ground, falling again before he reached the bottom and could cross the stream and get out into the lane. Out of breath, he rushed across the farmyard to the barn, scattering chickens and ducks as he went and dropping his shotgun by the barn door.

The fire had started to take hold of the barn, the dry hay acting as excellent fuel and the building was filled with thick smoke. Holding a handkerchief over his mouth, he moved carefully inside to locate the source of the fire and to see what of the building and its contents could be saved. But what had started it? There was no one here.

Starting to cough almost immediately in the thick acrid smoke, he was just able, through the tears in his eyes, to make out that the fire was still more smoke than flame, and could hopefully be controlled. He rushed out into the farmyard, grabbed a bucket almost overflowing with rainwater, and re-entering the barn threw the contents at the base of the flames. As the loudly hissing steam mixed with the smoke he caught sight of something out of the corner of his eye and was shocked to notice Jenny's body lying on the floor at the base of the ladder. He crouched down and gathering her up awkwardly in his arms, carried her out of the smoke and into the rain.

She looked unconscious, so he called her name, trying to wake her, and then shook her quite firmly by the shoulders, but in vain. Getting no response, he anxiously slapped her cheeks hoping she would open her eyes. She didn't. After a few minutes, now extremely concerned, he checked her wrist and neck for a pulse, his heart sinking and a lump coming into his throat when he couldn't find one. Kneeling on the ground in the rain and mud, he looked down sadly at her young face. The poor girl had been through enough; she didn't deserve this. Then he covered her with an old blanket he found just inside the barn, and with a heavy heart resumed his fire-fighting efforts until he was sure the fire was completely dowsed.

He then turned to deal with the sad problem of Jenny Tiley. She would need to be taken to the village and he needed to report what had happened. He couldn't carry her all the way to the village, for that he would need his trap, so he carried her across to the farmhouse porch and as gently as he could, laid her body gently on the ground.

Back at Manor Farm after a sorrowful walk which seemed to take far too long, he quickly explained to his shocked wife what had happened and hitched the horse to the trap. With Jenny aboard, he drove straight to Doctor Allerby's house. On his arrival, the two men carried Jenny's body into the doctor's consulting room, where after a brief examination, he pronounced her dead, and wrote out the necessary death certificate. Head injuries and smoke inhalation were the cause he gave George. Then he prescribed a much needed medicinal brandy for both of them, and advised George Wilkins to return home and have another before retiring to his bed.

"What of Constable Lodge?" the farmer asked.

"Don't worry about him," said Doctor Allerby. "I'll have someone fetch him. I'll explain I've sent you home and advise him to talk to you tomorrow. It's a sad business, though, George." The old farmer could do no more than nod his head. Jenny Tiley had been a popular young woman, even if some wicked tongues had turned against her.

Chapter Thirty-seven

Sitting in his study, appearing deeply engrossed in a book of sermons, but actually trying in vain to keep his mind from tomorrow's burial service for Jenny Tiley, Reverend Simpkins was almost relieved to hear a knock on his front door, as he wasn't expecting any visitors. With a grateful sigh, he closed his book and rose to answer the knocking, having to do it himself as his housekeeper Mrs Nesbitt was out in the village running errands for him. It was part of his chosen way of life to always be available to people, whatever time of day or night he was wanted, but there were times when he had to guiltily admit to himself that it was a little tiresome. But not this particular afternoon. A visitor would be welcome. It was however a surprise to find that Dr Allerby was on his doorstep when he opened the door. Although the two men were fairly well acquainted with each other, the doctor was far from being a frequent visitor to the rectory and the reverend, a healthy and robust man, was not one of the doctor's more frequent patients. After a few words of greeting, Reverend Simpkins invited the doctor in from the cold, relieved him of his coat, which he hung tidily on a coat stand and led him along the passage to his ever-untidy study.

Immediately they were seated, it seemed to the vicar that Doctor Allerby had something on his mind, something that was deeply bothering him. He politely declined the offer of a cup of tea, and thinking he might be in need of something a little stronger, the vicar offered him a glass of sherry, the fine qualities of which he was firmly believed would be of benefit to most stressful situations. The two men, glasses in hand, settled themselves sociably and informally in a pair of fireside chairs, facing the low welcoming fire which had been lit against the gloom of the November day. For a few minutes they chatted of the villagers and of various problems they had encountered which might be of interest to each other, but then both men fell silent. The vicar sat patiently waiting for the doctor to speak of what was on his mind, watching the other man slowly and almost painfully gathering his thoughts, although the doctor himself had been thinking of little else for some hours.

"There's something I wanted to talk about," the doctor began, almost warily.

"I guessed as much," replied the vicar, nodding. "Would you like more sherry before we start? As a doctor you should know it's very good for dry throats," he added, smiling, trying to make the doctor feel at ease with a little humour. As the vicar refilled their glasses on the other side of the room, Doctor Allerby continued.

"It's about Jenny Tiley," he said. The vicar turned sharply to face him, almost spilling the drinks. He passed the refill to Doctor Allerby.

"Jenny? I'm burying the poor young woman tomorrow," the vicar said sadly. "Is it something to do with the service?"

"I wish I could say no," the doctor said. He rubbed his chin uncomfortably. "This is all rather difficult, vicar. I'm not supposed to talk about patients and their state of health, although stretching a point, she's no longer my patient, is she?"

"What is said between a man and his vicar is only for the ears of God," the vicar said reassuringly, slightly worried by what he might be about to hear.

"You need have no doubts about my ability to keep a secret," he added, still with a gentle smile on his face. "If you want to talk, I'm willing to listen." There was another silence. The doctor seemed to be struggling with his conscience, the vicar thought.

"Martha Carter called me to see Jenny Tiley last week," the doctor began, looking into the fire, then paused.

"After Edward Tiley's funeral?"

"The day after, when we all found out Holt had left the village." The vicar nodded. He remembered his conversation with Nathan all too well.

"I thought you were seeing her regularly because of her illness?" he said.

"I was, but this visit turned out to be a little different. Martha wanted me to see Jenny because she was worried about reaction to the news, but that wasn't what Jenny wanted to talk about when I went into her room. What she wanted to talk about had nothing to do with her illness, or perhaps everything," he added enigmatically, pausing before almost blurting out his next words. "She thought she was having a baby."

"A baby?" Reverend Simpkins was slightly taken aback, genuinely surprised. The doctor nodded. "And was she?" Another nod, this time a little more reluctantly, while the doctor continued to stare into the low flickering flames of the fire and take small sips of his sherry. "So when she died..." The vicar's voice tailed off with the realisation of what had happened.

"The baby died with her," the doctor finished for him.

"Do you know who the father was?" the vicar asked, already knowing the answer, but dreading hearing it. It could only be one person.

"She told me, but I'd already guessed. She was too far into the pregnancy and her husband Edward was so badly injured that he wasn't physically capable of..." He let the sentence drop.

"Nathan Holt," said the vicar quietly. "Does he know?"

"No. It was after he left Smallbrook. A shame. I think if he'd known things might have turned out differently for Jenny and him."

"I agree. If he'd known, he certainly wouldn't have left, especially in the way that he did." He remembered the summer afternoon when he had said to Nathan and Jenny that God moves in mysterious ways. He certainly had over this whole sorry mess. "Does anyone else know?" he asked.

"No. Only myself, and now of course you." The two men looked at each other for what seemed to both of them to be an interminably long time. The vicar refilled their glasses for a second time, now thinking that they were both in need of it. Then the doctor continued. "I just thought you ought to know that tomorrow you're burying a woman who was carrying a baby," he said finally. "I just couldn't keep that to myself."

"You were quite right to tell me and it'll certainly be on my mind during the service, but God forgive me, I think we ought to keep this sad news to ourselves," said the vicar thoughtfully.

"You don't think we ought to contact Holt and tell him?" There was another long pause, finally broken by the vicar's answer.

"No, I don't. Nathan's gone back to the army and nothing can be done to change anything that's happened. What possible good could it do anybody to tell him?"

Chapter Thirty-eight

As the vicar had expected, Jenny Tiley's funeral was better attended than her husband's had been. She had made friends in the village; despite her being the subject of some gossip, and there was always gossip about a multitude of topics in a small village, people wished to pay their last respects. It was a grey cloudy, but still day; there was no rain or wind to disturb the flowers laid around the grave. Reverend Simpkins performed the simple service with a sad heart, feeling even more with the turn of events that he had in some way failed this poor unfortunate young woman. The knowledge of her unborn child hung heavy in his mind, eased only slightly by the silent prayer he'd offered up on its behalf.

The funeral over, the mourners dispersed to their homes, and, leaving the gravediggers, once again Harry Mason and his grandson, to their grim task, the vicar walked thoughtfully back to the vestry where he changed out of his robes. Then he sat for sometime alone in the empty church.

It was slow walk back to the the Rectory. Funerals always had this effect on him, so much more so when it was a young man or woman who'd had so much to look forward to in their lives. Of course, a child's funeral, all too regular an occurrence, was far worse. His study, when he finally lowered himself into his favourite armchair by the fire, seemed a refuge from his gloomy thoughts, and he buried himself in his books, preparing a sermon on grasping life's opportunities for the coming Sunday.

It was some time before he moved across the room to his desk and noticed an envelope lying on the corner, addressed simply to "Rev. Simpkins." He opened it immediately, and as he read the contents, settled back in his chair for a few moments before rising and crossing to the door of his study. He knew Mrs Nesbitt was in the kitchen preparing his tea and he called down the hallway for her. When she appeared, he asked her about the envelope.

"Oh yes, vicar. It was delivered just after you left for the church."

"Delivered?" he asked.

"Yes, by Little Johnny Williams who sometimes delivers those awful telegrams," she replied.

"Ah, the postmaster's son?"

"Yes, that's him."

"Did he say who gave it to him?" the vicar asked. She nodded.

"Yes, it was a man with a stick."

"A stick?" That puzzled him. She nodded again.

"Yes. Johnny said he thought it was the same man who was helping young Mrs Tiley at Smallbrook Farm."

"Nathan Holt," the vicar said. It was a statement, not a question, but the housekeeper nodded again in agreement. "That explains it," Reverend Simpkins continued. "But how would Nathan know of Jenny Tiley's death?" he was not expecting to receive an answer, as the question was mostly directed to himself, but as usual he was surprised by Mrs Nesbitt.

"Martha Carter, vicar. She wrote him a letter."

"A letter? How did she know where he was?"

"I'm not sure, sir. I think it was through the army." The vicar nodded and sighed. The military machine would not let go of their own. "Martha just thought he ought to know, sir. I hope she didn't do wrong?"

"Of course not. She was quite right. He did need to know." Satisfied, Mrs Nesbitt went back to her kitchen while Reverend Simpkins returned to his sermon more thoughtful than he had been. The contents of the envelope should have given him a clue: a handful of banknotes, and a short note which read: 'Please use this for a headstone for Jenny' and no signature. He stood and walked back to the armchair, knowing he couldn't concentrate on the sermon and sitting down again, he wondered where Nathan was and how badly he'd taken the news of Jenny's death.

The object of his thoughts was not as far away as he might have imagined and if the Reverend's study had overlooked the graveyard instead of his own overgrown garden and the brook, he would have seen Nathan standing over Jenny's grave. What he wouldn't have been able to see from that distance was the stream of tears flowing down the young man's face.

Nathan didn't stand there long, couldn't bring himself to. Just long enough to say goodbye and a quiet 'I love you' and place a single flower on the fresh soil. Then he turned towards the churchyard gate, and left.

Chapter Thirty-nine

Jack Evans liked the flour mill downstream from Dalton Combe; it had been one of his favourite places since he was a boy and his Bampi had brought him here fishing. The brook had been dammed centuries before to create a mill pond and mill race to power the now creaking old mill wheel and the water was bordered by reeds and willow trees dangling their delicate branches softly over its surface. The noisy rush of water through the sluice and down to the wheel had always relaxed him.

The water in the mill pond was deep, dark and dangerous. His mother, God rest her soul, had told him that often enough when he was a child, warning both him and his Bampi to be careful on their fishing expeditions. He missed them, his mother and his Bampi, both of whom were carried off in the awful 'flu epidemic that struck at the end of the Great War. He remembered somebody telling him, possibly his schoolteacher, or perhaps he'd read it himself in a newspaper, that more people died around the world as a result of the epidemic than had been killed in the war. And as his father had been one of the second group, the war had left him an orphan.

It was then that George Wilkins and his wife Alice had taken him in at Manor Farm. He'd already been working there and George, in his forthright way, had insisted that it was the only sensible thing to do. They'd treated him like the son they'd never had, and had proudly watched him develop into what he was now: a tall powerful young man of seventeen years of age. With a few hours to himself on a warm Sunday afternoon he'd got away from the farm and its seemingly never ending jobs and had decided on the mill pond, somewhere he'd been thinking about for some time.

It was the perfect place for him. He'd become a solitary and thoughtful young man as he grew from a child, and enjoyed his own company, although most of the time he didn't much enjoy the thoughts he was alone with. But it was the dreams he found harder to deal with, waking on many nights breathless, shaking and sweaty. Each time the same: blood, noise and screaming. And always the feeling of great unending sadness.

He settled himself on the bank, a favourite spot near the sluice and waterwheel, dropped what appeared to be a very heavy bag to the ground, where it fell with a thump, and laid a crude fishing pole and a small basket next to it. Then he watched the ducks floating almost effortlessly across the water, knowing that just below the surface, their webbed feet were going at nineteen to the dozen to give them that smooth motion. There was no one about, but the water wheel was turning sucking water at a ferocious rate through the sluice and he guessed that at least the miller, if not his assistants, were at work in the main building on this warm afternoon. He leaned back, lying full-length on the grass, looking up at the almost clear blue sky above him. He closed his eyes and listened to the sounds around him, sounds that were so familiar, so comforting. A wonderful summer afternoon that unfortunately reminded him of another summer afternoon from when he was a boy. An afternoon that he would have liked to forget, but that haunted him constantly and was the reason he was here today.

What had he been? About ten? Yes, because it was the summer he'd met Nathan Holt and started working for Mr Wilkins. He'd been running an errand for Mr Wilkins on a hot day, and had decided, with the innocent guile of a young boy, to return to Manor Farm by a very circuitous route that was well out of his way and just happened to include Smallbrook. There, he might be lucky enough to be given a refreshing glass of Mrs Tiley's delicious lemonade. He was always welcomed at Smallbrook, both by Mrs Tiley and by Nathan, with whom he missed working, but as he rushed breathlessly into the farmyard, neither of them were to be seen, although he could hear voices. They seemed to be coming from the kitchen, so that's where he went. Before he even reached the door though, the voices had become very loud, and it was Mrs Tiley and the other man, the one they said had come back from the dead. Then he heard screaming and swearing, swearing like he'd never heard before and hesitated on the threshold, but hearing an extra loud scream from Mrs Tiley had gone in just in time to see Edward Tiley swing a fist at Mrs Tiley and knock her to the floor, her head hitting the flagstones with a sickening thud. Seeing a revolver lying on the bedspread, and shocked by what he'd just seen, he acted as his heroes in the cheap cowboy books he loved to read would have reacted, and grabbed the gun, pulling the trigger. He'd never fired a gun, and the slam of the recoil hurt his arm so much that he dropped the weapon to the floor and cried out, but not before seeing the effect of his shot. He'd shot Edward in the head and there was blood everywhere. With Mrs Tiley appearing to be coming round he'd run from the house as fast as he could and up the hill to the copse above Smallbrook, where he'd lain hidden for the rest of the day, crying and shaking.

And that was what he suddenly found himself doing again, the memories too much, and he knew it was time. He'd had enough of the memories, the dreams, the guilt and the bad thoughts. He opened the bag,   took out a length of strong heavy twine and carefully re-tied the bag. Then he tied a noose with a slip knot and laid it out on the ground in front of where he was now sitting. After checking the knot worked smoothly, he fastened the loose end of the twine to the bag and then stood up and stepped inside the noose, which he then pulled tight around his ankles, re-checked the fastening to the bag and, picked it up, cradling it carefully in his arms. A short hobbling walk took him to the edge of the mill pond bank nearest the sluice and then he calmly stepped forward into the deep water, the bag acting as a weight and pulling him straight under the surface.

Chapter Forty

The letter stood out from all of the others. The correspondence he dealt with hour after hour and day after day arrived in great quantities in brown envelopes. This one was white and marked 'personal.' Idly wondering why it had arrived on his desk and not been given to him separately, Nathan carefully slit open the envelope, not recognising the handwriting of the address. It contained a short letter and a newspaper cutting which fell onto the desk as he unfolded and read the letter.

"Dear Nathan,

It has been a long time since we spoke and I hope you are keeping well. It took me rather a long time to discover your whereabouts, the army not being quite as helpful as they could have been. I realise events at Smallbrook and Dalton Combe are best left in the past, but something has happened that I felt it only right that you should be told about. I think the enclosed newspaper cutting speaks for itself.

Please forgive me for dragging up old memories, and may God be with you,

Reverend Simpkins."

Stationed now in the north of England, hundreds of miles and seven years away from the events of that summer of 1916, Nathan agreed that what had happened at Smallbrook should be left in the past, but as hard as he'd tried to put them out of his mind, it was something he just couldn't do. Intrigued as to what might have happened that Reverend Simpkins felt was so important, he unfolded the newspaper cutting. It gave no clue as to the newspaper it had been taken from, but did give a date of the fourth of June, 1923, nearly a month previously. He read it with growing shock. Tears welled up which he left to flow unchecked.

"Tuesday last. A coroner's hearing was held in the Municipal Rooms, River Street, concerning the body found in the mill pond of Straker's Mill, Dalton Combe. Readers will no doubt recall the circumstances reported in this paper last week. The body, identified as Mr Jack Evans of Manor Farm, Dalton Combe, a young man of seventeen years of age, was found to be blocking the sluice to the mill race, by miller Mr James Straker. The body had been weighed down with a bag of heavy rocks. Given these circumstances and the presence of a suicide note, also discovered by Mr Straker, who gave evidence at the hearing, Mr Justice Gwynne-Davies had no hesitation in giving a verdict of suicide whilst of unsound mind.

Readers may also be interested to hear that although Mr Justice Gwynne-Davies drew a veil over the contents of the suicide note, Mr Straker was happy to talk to this newspaper about what he had read. The note apparently made reference to Mr Evans' guilt about the tragic death of one Mr Edward Tiley at Smallbrook Farm, Dalton Combe some seven years ago. Mr Straker said he would never be able to forget the last words of the note: 'May God forgive me for what I did then, and for what I am about to do now.'"

Made in the USA
Charleston, SC
12 April 2016